RED ALERT

Strike Force [illegible] eapons snouting. They took [illegible] cking the aircraft, expendi[illegible] rt, trying to bring her d[illegible]
But [illegible] y. She tilted on a wing, a black [illegible] un's setting glow. Her propelle[illegible] ver. She banked superbly, levelled out, [illegible] d centre on their group.
"Not a sausage [illegible] Andy, ramming in a fresh magazine. He lift[illegible] his rifle again – and froze.
"Oh, my Christ!" he said.
Burnaby saw. There was time to feel sick right down to his stomach. He felt green.
From the Pucara spilled two cigar-shaped objects. They tumbled over in the air, seeming to take for ever as they floated down. The plane was a flashing blur of distorted colour. The two tanks were spinning towards the men below.
"Napalm!"

Also by Adam Hardy

Strike Force Falklands 1: Operation Exocet
Strike Force Falklands 2: Raider's Dawn

Adam Hardy

STRIKE FORCE FALKLANDS
3
RED ALERT

Futura
Macdonald & Co
London & Sydney

A Futura Book
First published in Great Britain in 1984 by
Macdonald & Co (Publishers) Ltd, London & Sydney

ISBN 0 7088 2543 5

Photoset in North Wales by
Derek Doyle & Associates, Mold, Clwyd
Printed in Great Britain by
Collins, Glasgow.

Futura Publications
A Division of
Macdonald & Co (Publishers) Ltd
Maxwell House
74 Worship Street
London EC2A 2EN

A BPCC plc Company

CHAPTER ONE

The two aircraft whistled by, a scant dozen feet above the sea. The water beneath them glittered in the sunlight like an expressway, hard as stone and cold as death. Every now and then the planes were forced to jink sideways to avoid a wave which would have smashed them into the sea.

Cramped into the tiny cockpit of his Douglas A4 Teniente Alonzo Mancuso felt so alert and aware of everything going on around him that he seemed to have ascended into a higher plane of living. He could feel the aircraft as an extension of his body, every tremor vibrating directly in his own nervous system. But if he *did* ascend to a higher plane British radar would pick him up like a fly on flypaper.

Across off his port wingtip his wingman and friend Rafael held his plane down, scraping the wavetops. The sensation of speed and onward rushing adventure had to be channelled as his instructors had taught him, filed away where it belonged.

As for fear – sure, he'd been scared stupid on the first missions until the action started. Then there was no time to be frightened.

The little A4 bucked like a bronco of the pampas as turbulence buffeted her. Flying was a sweating business this low down, skimming over the sea, fighting the controls all the way.

The technical boys back at base had worked out the calculations of payload and fuel, and the Douglas flew sluggishly with the weight of bombs slung beneath her wings.

"Keep to your headings and courses and don't deviate," the *jefe del escuadron* had warned his pilots. "Your fuel will see you through with enough reserve."

The pilots had nodded sagely, making notes on their knee pads.

"If you *chicos* do silly things – you'll ditch."

Ditching in the South Atlantic was a prospect to be avoided.

Constantly, working to a pattern, Mancuso scanned the horizon, checked his instruments, made sure he was holding his heading, checked the compass, and then scanned the horizon again.

A tiny black speck was one thing he did not wish to see out there.

The pilots of the Fuerza Aerea Argentina were in Harrier country.

Teniente Alonzo Mancuso could fly. He was aware that he and his comrades were superb pilots. Their training had been thorough and dedicated. This mission was the culmination of years of effort. He had been through the Escuela De Aviacion Militar in Cordoba, had studied in the same rooms in which the Brigadier had worked. Although some of his friends had been trained by Israeli and French instructors, flying Mirages and Neshers (which the Fuerza Aerea called Daggers) he still fancied his luck. Everyone knew that the Israelis were among the most professional and highly experienced pilots in the world. It remained to be seen if the RAF and the RN pilots were as good as they were cracked up to be.

Already, in the first days, Mancuso had lost friends.

Now, on this most important of days, he was imbued with a burning determination.

Today, Tuesday, 25th May, 1982, the anniversary of the day Argentina threw off the yoke of foreign domination, Independence Day, would see the British Task Force finally crushed, sunk, ruined.

Orders called for the first attacks to be made against military targets. Sink the warships – then the transports and supply ships would be at the mercy of the Argentine planes.

Mancuso had confessed his secret disappointment to Rafael after the initial attacks on the invasion force.

"I'd like to have sent a bomb down *Canberra*'s funnel!"

Rafael had laughed in his cheeky way, and replied: "Don't worry! We'll sink all the frigates and destroyers – then we'll capture *Canberra*!"

With a thump of blood Mancuso spotted the low dark streak ahead.

The Islands!

He flashed on, a fleet shape, skimming the sea.

The operational plan called for an approach over West Falkland and then a sharp turn so that the aircraft could attack down San Carlos Water, out of the sun. Then another sharp turn away and a swift flight home. By using the land to cover their approach, the planes gained the benefit of radar clutter on the British screens.

Other squadron aircraft would turn north to tangle with the British picket ships. Rumour had it that there was a big fish on offer today. That would be the job for the Armada, and the Navy fliers might slap in an Exocet where it would do the most good.

If the chance to hit *Hermes* or *Invincible* came Mancuso's way, he'd lap it up like a cat licking cream.

The flyers of *los halcones* had already sunk HMS *Brilliant* and seriously damaged other ships, and sunk two frigates. The British were taking a hammering and Mancuso, for one, felt that the air war was being pressed on to victory.

With *Sheffield* sunk, the British could surely not sustain these grievous wounds. They must cry quarter, pack up, and go home.

Time telescoped.

Mancuso's reactions were purely automatic.

He became, if that were possible, even more a part of his aircraft, his brain controlling all the intricate fabric of destruction.

The Ferranti ISIS D126R sight: *on*.

The two 20mm cannon safety: *off*.

Bomb panel: *live*.

The harness for the rotten ejector seat that more often than not wouldn't work properly tightened with the hope it would not have to be used ...

Now the land flashed past beneath his wings.

Brown and green and streaks of white, rushing past.

The feel of speed and movement and lightness, buoyed up, hurtling on, the glimpse of water ahead ...

Long grey shapes, lethal and waiting in deadly ambush – the ships of the Royal Navy.

Abruptly-red dots, sparkling beads of light, rising in strings ... Between each tracer round the unseen but mortally dangerous shells whickered past. Off to the side the long white trail spearing upwards told Mancuso that a missile had been fired. He hoped Rafael was safe.

The Douglas screamed on, speeding over the dazzling scene spread out below, travelling fast, giving only a fragmentary glimpse of the action.

The air filled with flak. Other missiles rose.

The A4 whistled past, turning with a sure and incisive swirl of wings. A small insect-like shape of hurtling speed and power, it dived for the final run-in to the target.

Time foreshortened. The target was selected in the approach. Mancuso tilted the plane, lined up, bore down.

Now, as the bull-fighters said, was the moment of truth.

The aftermath of that dizzying greying of vision as the

G-suit fought centrifugal forces in the turn left him with the feeling that he was going in dead on line. Across the stretch of water the outline of the ship swelled as he screamed in for the attack.

A frigate, low and lean with that fat raked funnel, was shooting at him. A twinkling of fire along her sides, smoke whiffing away, the beads of tracer lifting …

Closer and closer …

Head down, bore everything but the vital moment when he must drop his bombs …

The frigate filled his vision. He felt no animosity towards her or her men; she was just a target, a bulls-eye to be hit fair and square. He knew the moment had come; sights exact. He pressed the tit.

The bombs leaped away and, like a fractious colt, the Douglas lifted and leaped in her turn, freed of the load.

Now he had to turn the plane, swing her away from the bomb blast, scream over the frigate so low he might clip an aerial, part a wire. A jumbled impression of the ship below, flashing away so fast it appeared a mere phantasm. He had to curve the Douglas, head her away, keep low and fast, and streak for the land.

Operating at this range from base there was precious little time to loiter. He knew his bombs had hit.

He knew it.

He felt success in his bones, felt it in his blood.

Bits and pieces of the frigate flew into the air as he passed, smashed free by the force of his bombs.

Now he was in a gut-wrenching turn, pelting straight for the land, on course for home.

If a Harrier latched on to him now …

No.

No, Teniente Alonzo Mancuso was superbly confident, certain, sure.

He had carried out another successful mission.

His bombs had hit a British frigate, he was on his way

back to base, and no damned Harrier would ever catch him now.

Lance Corporal Taylor stuck his spade into the peaty ground and shovelled dirt. The spade came out with a loud sucking sound. Spider Taylor looked into the beginnings of the hole with an expression of the utmost disgust.

"Sod this for a game of chess." He glared at Trampas, who straightened up from his hole with an expression of exasperation. "Let's get up a bit higher, for Pete's sake!"

"Gimme a fishing rod and line and I'd pull our supper out of my hole," said Trampas.

Both men stared glumly at the water rapidly seeping into the scrapes they had begun.

Sergeant Major Andrew Stubbs walked across from his own scrape. Everyone wore camouflage clothing, the DPM in some cases making them show up more than they should against the Falklands colour schemes.

"All right," said Andy, "Let's get up to that little ridge. The water can't follow us up *that* high!"

"Wanna bet?" said Trampas ominously.

Laconic to the point of monosyllabic conversations, the men of Special Strike Force now and then let it all hang out, let their hair down, let the language flow. When you dug yourself a hide to get well down into and take cover from the Argie aeroplanes, you didn't want to rest your butt in water. No sir. Everything was cold and damp enough as it was, not that mere climatic privations affected the men of Strike Force as they might personnel of other formations. Just that warfare demanded that one do things the right way.

And sharing a hole with fifty gallons of water was not on.

When Strike Force was out on an op, they'd stand for hours on end up to their necks in water. That was just a part of the mystique that set them apart from the rest of the British Army – or most of it. No. No, when they were preparing for a fresh operation they valued what comfort they could scratch together.

Humping their enormous loads – jaguar packs, ammo, missile-launchers, jimpys, radios, grub – they started off up the slope. Around them the day smiled pleasantly enough, although there had been quite a few air reds already. These Argie pilots really had guts. They'd pass on through intense flak to reach the warships out in San Carlos Water, and the gunline in the Sound.

During the last attack, Strike Force had been able to look as the air battle developed. The Argie planes screamed low over the water, and then they'd spill their bombs, loose off their cannon, and go screeching away. The amount of flak and missile fire that went up after them was phenomenal.

Many were shot down.

So far the air strikes had not occured too near SSF. Captain Edward Parkes, RAMC, universally known as Sawbones, fretted. Here he was, probably about to become vitally involved in keeping the men's feet clear of rot and fungus and trench foot, when men were being blown up and burned and the doctors over there would vastly welcome his help. But Sawbones was a member of Strike Force. His priority was keeping the men of his own unit fit and in action.

Andy Stubbs was in no mood to hang about.

"Come on," he shouted. "Speed o' light. Speed o' light."

"What the hell," said Spider. "We ain't back in Catterick, are we?"

The habitual use of nicknames in Strike Force meant that the personnel meshed on the intimate man-to-man level of equals in combat and experience; it also served to act as shorthand, speedily linking groups and individuals, and also, to a great degree, gave security to signals.

"He'll be on about our feet not touching the ground next," commented Corporal Thwaite with mock gloom.

"Yes," said Corporal Hammond. "But he can't say much about getting our hair cut, now can you, Andy?"

"A right hairy bunch," said Andy, who as a WOII with a reverence for his parent unit, the 2nd Foot Guards, never ceased to amaze himself at the uncouth hairiness of this bunch of Strike Force maniacs with whom nowadays his enitre life was wrapped up.

The men clambered up the slope like the apes on Gibraltar. Lieutenant Charlie Mainwaring, universally known as Q, busied himself checking that nothing was overlooked or left behind.

Watching the activity, actively concurring in the move to higher ground, Captain Tom Burnaby felt a bubbling sense of freedom. He'd been pitchforked into command of Strike Force through odd circumstances not unfamiliar in any soldier's career in action, and he'd had his problems.

Major Dan Granville, the Old Man, had personally selected every member of Strike Force. The lads worshipped him. He'd been badly hit over on the mainland, and Guy, the second in command, had gone down with infected guts. So that left Tom Burnaby holding the baby. So far he'd coped. They'd done what the high brass had asked them to do, done it handsomely. And now the way the men talked gave Burnaby a tremendous kick.

They'd never reveal themselves like this to anyone not of Strike Force.

To the outside world in the person of those people with whom they came into contact who knew they were members of Strike Force, they presented that hard, taciturn, almost mean facade that was fast becoming their mystique. It was no good SSF deploring this. They *were* like that when it came to push of pike. That they were also human beings appeared to be a secret only they knew.

In the lee of the ridge conditions were decidedly better.

The scrapes, although damp and unfriendly, did not fill with water the moment spades came out. Stores built up into windbreaks. Ponchos were spread. Spider started to mutter about a brew up.

Spread out below them the water and the ships might have appeared toylike. The scene might have seemed normal.

It did not.

The ships of the Task Force were unloading as fast as they could. Ceaseless activity testified to the herculean efforts being put into getting stores ashore before they were all blown out of the water and to Kingdom Come.

The loggies were earning their crusts today all right.

Logistics Regiment personnel worked damned hard. If they got killed they died like anyone else.

The Navy had brought the marines and soldiers to the land. The ships had to remain in position in order to put up their umbrella of flak until the army got their Rapier anti-aircraft missile batteries functioning.

And the Argentine pilots stuck stubbornly to bombing the warships. A number of calculated attacks had been put in on the marine and para positions to negate that first reading of the situation; but it was clear enough that the Argentine thinking indicated that if the warships were sunk or severely damaged then the rest of the force, afloat and starving and out of ammo-ashore, could be dealt with at leisure.

Strike Force, settling in some way away from the rest of the marines and army, were cut off from casual contact. That was the way they liked it. The Whizz Kid went past draped in his infernal devices, and Burnaby walked downslope to bring up the last of the loads.

Everyone chipped in in Strike Force.

Distantly, he heard the shouts.

"Air Red! Air Red!"

In the next second, or so it seemed, the Argie aircraft were there.

"There they are!" yelled Hammer. He threw down the pack he was lifting and tried to burrow under it.

Burnaby felt the laughter in him as Hammer surfaced, swearing, and grabbed for his rifle.

"Never hit 'em with this at that range – "

"No." Burnaby hefted the Blowpipe that was his last load. The thing weighed a ton and was big and clumsy; but it worked fine. It was not popular with the men on account of weight and cumbersomeness. Q had brought a couple along from Strike Force stores because Q believed in Being Prepared.

"While we're hanging about here I don't want any Argie squirting up my rear and me with nothing to shoot back," had been Q's perfectly reasonable philosophy.

Burnaby switched on, checked, primed, made sure the missile launcher was prepared as Q hoped. He lifted it to his shoulder.

"You'll get your fool head blown off, Tom!" yelped Hammer.

Swinging in low over the water, a couple of aircraft looked small and somehow incongruously like stones flung by boys across a pond. Those planes were McDonnell Douglas A4P's – Skyhawks – flogged off cheap to Argentina when the US Navy had grown out of them. They were A4B models upgraded by better sights and equipment into the P model. They were not flung stones. They were not darting insects. They were deadly bombers that had already sunk British ships. Bits of *Antelope* were still out there, bows jutting out of the water and indelibly reminding Burnaby of that earlier *Invincible*, the battle cruiser that got her come-uppance at Jutland.

The planes screeched along, their browny-green colour indicating they were Fuerza Aerea and not Aviacion Naval. He lined up on the nearest, hoping the Blowpipe had the range. He centred the sights and pressed the trigger and let fly.

He held on, watching, holding the track dead.

The missile fizzed away towards the speeding Skyhawk.

Teniente Alonzo Mancuso's elation soared as the Douglas A4 formated off his port wingtip.

That was Rafael.

Good! Rafael had come through, just as he had himself. Now they were tearing towards the land, keeping low, seeking the friendly cover the ground would give them against the British radar. There were no Harriers. Mancuso could feel everything; there were as yet no deflating after-effects of reaction. He still had the long haul back to base; that would pass, that would pass.

Rafael kept perfect formation. Mancuso was a little inland of his wingman. The water flipped away astern and they screamed over the browny-orangey land with its scraps of greenery and scatterings of white rocks.

In only moments they would be well away.

The ships had all ceased shooting at him, left well astern. Now there was only the spit of land then he would

CHAPTER TWO

The Skyhawk exploded into an envelope of fire.

Chunks of burning débris flew off. A massive ball of fire roared on, swirling, spewing flames, and smashed headlong into the soggy peat of the Falklands.

A column of greasy black smoke rose into the bright air.

"Poor sod," said Hammer.

Burnaby lowered the Blowpipe launcher. His face showed no expression. He felt entirely different from any way he had felt before in the face of inflicted violence.

Hell – he felt as though he'd stepped on an insect, a beetle, and lifted his foot to reveal the crushed black and red mess beneath.

The other Skyhawk barrelled on.

Q came back, squat and chunky, a human dynamo.

"Poor bugger," said Hammer, varying the words if not the sentiment.

"If his stupid government hadn't tried to pinch what wasn't theirs, and do the dirt on folk who want to stay British, that poor little devil could still be happily flying around Buenos Aires right now."

"Amen," said Andy, joining the group, all staring at the ominous black column of smoke.

"They hadn't the nous to think like that in BF," pointed out Burnaby. "And now they're finding it out in DF."

"Yes, well," added Andy. "There's no AF for that poor sod."

BF – Before Falklands. DF – During Falklands. AF – After Falklands.

Life changed, in a twinkling, in the pressure of a finger on a trigger, on the strike of a missile – life changed.

"You could say that in BF – " Q looked down over the water and the ships and up and around again. " – that we all were."

There was no answer to that.

Life went on – on this anniversary day in particular.

"Some Special Forces," went on Q in his bulldoggish way, "have finagled themselves Yankee Stinger anti-aircraft missiles."

"You don't mean you were beaten to it, Q?" Andy was relishing the unusual situation. Stinger was much the same as Blowpipe but a lot easier to manage.

"Strings in high places, my old son, strings in high places."

"We'll manage with what we have." Burnaby turned away from the rising column of smoke. He felt that, had he not looked away, his stare would have become hypnotic, that he'd have spent the rest of his life basilisk-fixed on the pyre of a gallant Argentinian pilot. "As soon as Smyjo gets back we'll be off. The choppers are all arranged."

That was a source of great satisfaction. The men of Strike Force could yomp, tab or hack their way across the hellfire plains of the damned if they had to. They quite liked to be carried into action in luxury.

The scrapes were dug into slightly more commodious holes in the lee of the ridge. Put a British soldier down somewhere and he'll dig himself into the ground like a mole. Just common sense – especially here where the Argie planes kept up a furious assault along Bomb Alley.

Spider got on with brewing up. Rations were broken

out. Chomping away on chicken supreme, Burnaby reflected that the poor Argie pilot had just been unlucky.

The Blowpipe aiming unit's auto-gathering device had brought the Skyhawk into the centre of the monocular sight's vision, and the thumb-controlled joystick guided the Blowpipe perfectly. There was only a thirty degree tolerance. A few degrees either side and the Skyhawk would have been clear and flying for home.

Poor sod ...

The slope of the hill in the lee of the ridge looked rather like a jumble sale on a rainy afternoon, or Steptoe and Son's yard, or perhaps like the surface of the warrens of cybernetic rabbits. Special Strike Force – SSF – might only be staying for a short time until they lifted out by helo; still they dug themselves in nice and tidy.

The day wore on, this special day in which everyone felt the Argies must try a big push to make something out of their tattered national honour.

As Andy mentioned to Burnaby: "Funny the Argies weren't waiting on the beach. Or they don't come storming over them hills. They can't just be sitting on their fat behinds back at Stanley."

"I expect their general knows what he's up to, even if we don't."

Andy cocked his head, his face like a craggy granite outcrop.

"Sounds like another Air Red."

"Yep."

This time the Argentine planes, Daggers and Skyhawks, flashed over the water, skimming insects of death, away from the positions of Strike Force. The men watched impotently as the air filled with smoke and the white trails of missiles, the flash of wings, and the sky cracked with the bang and bluster of explosions.

Standing watching, Burnaby was ready to dive headlong into his hole at the first sight or sound of a hostile heading their way. The attackers bored in with enormous courage. Bomb Alley turned into Death Alley.

"That fellow you nobbled, Tom," said Andy, not looking at Burnaby but out over the water. "Did you see his bombs?"

"No."

"They hit that ship all right, fair and square. But I don't think they could have exploded."

"Well, she's still out there shooting like a firecracker on the fifth of November."

"Right. I reckon the Argies are using duff bombs."

"That's what comes from buying second hand, perhaps. Perhaps they're not fused right."

"Thank the Lord for whatever it is."

Rapier batteries were now able to go into action and the guided missiles climbed away, fizzing their smoke trails and depending on the judgement of the operator might bring down an enemy plane. Burnaby had nurtured the vague belief that guided missiles never missed, until he'd talked to an RAF fellow and come away with that illusion shattered.

"A Very pistol, old boy. If that's all you've got!"

Burnaby saw no indication that the Argies shot any form of chaff or heat-decoy to fool the British missiles.

The raid petered out. The landing areas came to life again and the helicopters popped up from their hiding places.

"All for what?" said Andy.

"What?"

"That bloke you got. There's his target, she's been hit but she's okay."

"Good."

"Sure, Tom, sure good. But – but that young idiot gave his life for nothing."

Andy looked his usual grim, trim, competent self. A man to have at your side in times of trouble and in times of celebration. One of the very best. Burnaby would trust him with the last waterbottle in the desert.

So? What was Andy on about?

Burnaby had not envisaged his own private feelings of distancing from the violence habitual to an action-front soldier as being shared by many, if any at all, of his comrades. He knew he thought far too much about things best left unthought-about.

"He must have been a volunteer," went on Andy. "You don't get conscripts flying planes."

"True."

"Poor sod."

"That's what Hammer said."

"And now he's dead – for nothing."

Andy stomped off to make sure that young rip Spider Taylor was conducting himself as befitted a Soldier of the Queen. To the sergeant major there was absolutely no incongruity in the juxtaposition of the concepts of, on the one hand the image of a red-coated Soldier of the Queen, and on the other of guided missiles and jet aircraft. Burnaby stared after Andy and shivered.

If Andy got himself killed the Pearly Gates were in for a riotous ten minutes when he arrived.

The fragmentary conversation, with so much unsaid, reminded him of Naomi. He'd had to go a long way towards the brink of spelling it out for her.

Of course, he'd been young then, studying like a swot to get on in the Signals. Naomi, one of those lanky girls with fashionable giglamps and blue stockings, had been hovering on and hovering off, and he'd been frustrated and she'd brought up the subject, not without distaste, of his chosen profession.

"A soldier, Tom? But you kill people."

He hadn't thought too much about that side of the business.

"Well, someone has to – if they're trying to kill me and

rape you."

"Tom!"

"Well, you know what I mean."

She'd let him walk her home from night school – arty crafty folk-weaving – and she contrived to wiggle away when he tried to put his arm around her waist.

"Wait until – you're so impatient!"

"Anyway," he went on, talking to keep his mind off the feel of her waist and the firm softness of the bulge above. "Anyway, soldiers get killed too." Then, with a cunning stroke of pleading, an appeal to her to lower her defences, he added: "I could get killed, easy."

She walked on, her long legs convenient to pace alongside, and she tossed her head in the street lamps' glow.

"And I'm supposed to feel sorry?"

Then he spoke, and the words came sounding up from an unsuspected well within him, astounding him as though he spoke with tongues.

"That's the difference between professionals and conscripts. Anyone who joins the army, volunteer or conscript, has to anticipate that, well, one day he might get killed. The professional knows that no matter how good he is, one day he may have cold-bloodedly to lay down his life in the course of his duty."

She'd stopped at that, perhaps dimly perceiving a little of what went to make up this man Tom Burnaby. Her lips looked purple in the street light. When they walked on she did not wiggle away when he put his arm about her waist.

Later on, outside her front garden gate under the plane tree, her bra came off. But she resolutely refused to allow explorations below the equator. Going back to barracks, Tom Burnaby reflected that he must be picking up more from Sergeant McArdle than he suspected. McArdle's quotations were by way of being famous in the corps.

So, here he was, a three-pip captain in R. Sigs, appointed to temporary command of Special Strike Force, burrowing into a damp and uncomfortable hillside on the Falklands.

The Argentine raids kept up. Occasionally they struck for the marine positions, and a hail of machine gun fire rose. Those bootnecks were loosing off with their SLRs, too. Burnaby felt a nasty twinge at what the quartermasters were saying at the sight of all those stores being loosed off so recklessly.

Well, Strike Force would not be hanging about the beachhead much longer. The helicopters would take them inland to their objectives where they would make life miserable for the enemy; always, of course, assuming there were enemy to be found up there.

Spider was nattering on about having another brew up. Water was in chronically short supply, and the Arctic rations, dehydrated, were going to prove a problem if the situation did not improve. The General Service rations, in tins, might come into their own.

Lieutenant Christopher Smythe-Jones showed up at last. He came striding up the hill, his lithe limber freedom of movement shifting him along effortlessly. A member of the Guards Brigade, Smyjo, big and powerful, utterly cocksure, a tremendous fighter, a man to have at your side when death beckoned.

And, of course, Burnaby just couldn't make himself like the big guardsman. That was nonsensical, he knew that, despairingly aware of his own irrational attitude. But Smyjo was so – so – so absolutely marvellous he got right up Burnaby's hooter.

Burnaby looked surprised.

"Thought you'd be bringing yourself in the choppers Smyjo."

Smyjo was not smiling.

"Chopper," he said. "Singular."

It was important for Burnaby to hold himself in check. He must not say the wrong word, must not make the wrong gesture. Something had happened. Smyjo looked bloated, as though indigestion had caught him betwixt wind and water with no lavatory in sight.

Some of the others came up, quietly, standing in their loose, relaxed poses. The day, this special day, would soon be gone.

"Called at HQ." Smyjo had contacts there that owed nothing to any military network.

Everyone waited. They all knew that something had happened.

"The Argies were after *Hermes*. They sank *Coventry* – "

A hiss of indrawn breath from more than one man in that circle of Strike Force. Burnaby waited, graven.

"They didn't get *Hermes*, or *Invincible*. No. No they got *Atlantic Conveyor*."

No one spoke.

Smyjo looked around, knowing what each of them wanted to ask.

"Yes, there were casualties; but, thank God, not too many."

"Any at all's bad," said Andy.

"*Atlantic Conveyor*." Q looked sick. "She was stuffed with kit!"

There was no disguising the seriousness of this tragedy. Good men had been killed. Tons of stores had been destroyed. HMS *Coventry* – sunk!

"*Atlantic Conveyor* had four Chinooks," Q said in his bulldoggish way, brushing aside anything else in this disaster to concentrate on what immediately affected Strike Force and his responsibilities. "And Wessexes, and Harriers. Any news on those, Smyjo?"

"The Harriers were already operating and I believe one Chinook was saved. All the rest have been kyboshed."

"Hell and damnation."

Burnaby had to get a grip on this situation at once.

"We figured we were lucky to get a helo to carry us forward," he said, speaking in a mild yet crisp tone that he knew would make the lads brace up. "We can always hack it. If we have one chopper we're in luck. We can only hope the loss of life was not too great, feel damn sorry for the lads who got killed and those who are injured, and kit ourselves up ready for the off."

He looked around at Strike Force.

"If the Argies think they've won a great victory and we'll skulk off now – they've got another think coming."

CHAPTER THREE

Burnaby slung his jaguar pack down alongside Andy's and turned back to the helicopter. Everyone took a hand in humping stores in Strike Force. The chopper, the single helicopter made available to them and damned lucky they were to get her, was loaded to the gunwales carrying far more than her design specifications had envisaged. The night held enough hours for her to make the necessary number of flights from base to the cluster of rocks at the foot of Point 205 in the north of the island.

The wind plucked at Burnaby and the night held a frosty glint, the stars burning sparkle-bright overhead. If anyone was up there on the hill they might just catch the distant sound of the helicopter's engine and vanes; they most certainly would not see a blind thing of the arrival of Strike Force.

Earlier, special forces reconaissance patrols had established an Argentine presence on the hill. Whether or not the Argies were still there was a question that in its answer would provide even more questions.

Smyjo had no doubts.

"Winkle 'em out," he said, brusquely confident. "As soon as they see us, they'll run."

"Like their aeroplane pilots?"

"Not the same, old boy, not the same."

Andy said: "If they're conscripts, my money's on

Smyjo. If they're not, then – "

"Oh, come on, Andy!" Smyjo lifted his eyebrows in mock disbelief. "You don't think the Argies would stick decent troops out here, do you?"

Burnaby wasn't so sure.

"If they think we're coming this way they could well stick a battalion of their paras or marines out here to check us. Hell – who can fathom what they're thinking over there in Stanley?"

"Beats me, old boy."

Q stomped up. He did not make a formal report that all stores were down, and no one thought to ask. If the stores had been short of the smallest item, then Q would have had something to say.

Smyjo nodded in that semi-regal way of his that so infuriated Burnaby, and went on: "But as to sticking a battalion of decent chaps out here. H'm. Not on, my old son, not on."

Q flopped down and pointed out an item of information unknown as yet to the Argentines.

"They don't know they've clobbered a whole fleet of helicopters."

"So they won't be expecting us to walk all the way to Stanley on our flat feet. So?"

"So maybe their defence isn't as daft as you suggest."

Smyjo sniffed at that. Burnaby – wisely – refrained from comment.

Spider in his raffish way said: "If I was trying to stop us I'd have done it by now. Shoved us back into the sea."

Lawless smiled evilly at his oppo.

One or two others voiced their opinions. A kind of half-speed Chinese Parliament eventually came to the conclusion that no one knew the score.

The mission, in essence, was simple.

Just keep the Argies occupied, make them think they were being assaulted in this area by at least a half-battalion strength, knock 'em off balance, hit here and hit there and don't keep still.

Easy enough to spell out.

As before in Strike Force's fortunes, carrying out the task was an entirely different matter.

The concealing hours of darkness were slipping away. Strike Force had to be in position and invisible by first light.

"I'll get off, then, Tom."

"Right, Smyjo."

Smyjo and his patrol would range ahead, checking the ground, staking out a line, and select the best possible position in which to construct the first hides and then the base. The rest would follow and consolidate.

Every man of Strike Force implicitly trusted every other man. There was no room for the petty squabbles and animosities of other units. As Burnaby had already surmised, the dubious advantage of an extra edge imparted to a group by mutual antipathy was too expensive, was counter-productive. Psychologists might postulate that rivalry generated by dislike could drive men on; in Burnaby's experience it could lead to expensive mistakes.

This, of course, made all the more infuriating his irrational antipathy towards Smyjo. The big guardsman was a splendid fellow. No doubt of it. Why, then, this dragging feeling of inferiority, this sense that in Smyjo's shoes Burnaby would make a mess of life?

He watched Smyjo and Smartie, with Acting Sergeant Sidney Hodge – known as Splodge – and L/Cpl David Jones – known as Taff – as they vanished into the darkness.

Burnaby turned away and put his mind to organizing the rest of the lads into the most efficient system of transport to bring the supplies up to the base Smyjo would select. As he did so a scorching picture of Miss

Claire Havisham shocked through him. The vision came from nowhere, flamed for a heart-beat in his brain, and vanished.

Tears glimmered on her bruised cheeks in the headlamps' glare. Bruises marked her, blue-black, her lip was split, her clothes ripped. She staggered and fell.

Burnaby in the chill Falklands' wind came to his senses, shivering.

"You all right, Tom?"

His voice replied before he thought, sharp and yet growly.

"Sure, Hammer, sure."

"Right."

The Whizz Kid went past, draped in his evil devices, and Burnaby was back in the Falklands.

Up ahead, Smyjo led his four-man patrol with the caution a Red Indian would envy. Tracking over the ground was treacherous. The earth itself was more often soft and peaty than otherwise; yet areas of hardness lay here and there, and there were always rocks and stones to trip the unwary. A kicked stone, the clatter of a rock, would alert even the most dull of conscripts on sentry go.

The hill lifted against the stars, a dark humped shape, at one with the night.

Finding a ravine of the sort favoured by Srike Force consumed precious time. Eventually Smyjo settled on a slot of land topped by a clutter of rocks and sparse and bristly vegetation. There wasn't a single damned tree in the whole of the islands. He dumped his kit and flipped on his Scimitar pocket radio.

"Tom? Tom?"

Burnaby's voice came back, flat and tinny yet perfectly audible.

"Here."

"Found a spot. Making a recce. Splodge and Taff will guide you in."

"Check."

With that Smyjo touched Smart on the arm and the two men, gripping their weapons, stripped to battle kit, started off towards the right flank.

The intensity of the training undergone by personnel of Strike Force and the fraught experiences which they had endured tended to make them taciturn on patrol, curt, perhaps a trifle over-harsh. They spoke only when necessary. On patrol you were all eyes and ears and nose, feeling the air, the ground, sorting away information and deducing what was going on around you.

Failures in these circumstances usually ended up dead.

Creeping at an angle up a little slope that would lead to another declivity and another slope, Smyjo halted.

Instantly, Smart dropped flat where he kept station a few paces off and to the rear with Smyjo always in sight. The wind scoured along and the grasses whispered secrets to one another.

Up ahead a rock clattered.

To himself, Smart said: "A pound to a pinch of, that's a sheep."

Working with careful patient attention, the two men worked around the source of the noise.

When they closed in Smart smirked to himself.

"Poor little thing," said Smyjo. "It's lost."

Sentimentality was perfectly all right – in its place. Here, on the bleak hillsides of the Falklands, it also had its place – but at the right time.

Smyjo started off again, followed by Smart.

The big guardsman allowed himself the remark: "I feel sorry for that sheep if Q gets his hands on her."

As Strike Force rapidly found out, there was a drastic shortage of sheep anywhere near where soldiers happened to go. That this indicated a modicum of distrust of soldiers was by the by. The islanders were common-sense folk, and the kelpers simply made sure their sheep were not too obvious. This sensible course of action may have begun with the Argentine invasion and now simply continued as a habit; it did mean the troops could get on with killing one another instead of chasing potential lamb chops all over the camp.

The two men scouted across the front of the position, checking that the Argies had not established any forward posts that would prove embarrassing to Strike Force.

They found not a human soul.

By the time they wormed their way back to the gulley the rest of the force had arrived, and Smyjo was able to tell Burnaby that the front was clear.

"Maybe the whole damn hill is clear," said Burnaby unpleasantly.

"If it is," Andy chipped in, "we'll have to chase the Argies that much farther, that's all."

Dawn found Strike Force set up, the main base established yet invisible, four-man patrols out, two men up and two in relief, at forward posts. Strike Force was in business.

A day of observation would follow, a day that might appear to hold no excitement. This was the stuff of special forces operations. From what was observed and noted this day would follow the lurid actions of the night.

Lurid only, as Burnaby wryly reflected, if there were any Argies up there at all.

CHAPTER FOUR

There *were* hostiles on the hill.

During the day the men of Strike Force in their observation hides spotted and logged the Argentine movements.

The general consensus of opinion was that there were two companies on the hill. Perhaps a reinforced company with support weapons hunkered on the feature; either way, the odds were the sort that no commander would take unless he was suicidally inclined. Or – unless he was cunning and devious and prepared to make advantages where none apparently existed.

During the morning a pair of Pucaras flew over, propellers whirring, wings slanting in the still bright sunlight. Burnaby was confident that they wouldn't spot any members of Strike Force.

That was not the problem.

He was sitting in the scrape he and Andy had gouged from the earth, rocks piled apparently haphazardly around the edges, a poncho stretched across the top. The place was damp – of course – and cold, yet it was more of a palace than many a special forces soldier could expect on an op.

No – the problem was just how much of a noise to make before the Argentine positions.

He glanced across at the Blowpipe against the earthen wall.

One Pucara lost to the enemy would be one aircraft less. His job was to baffle them, make them jumpy, soften them up. Maybe …

The decision was made for him as the Pucaras kept out of range. That this was purely by chance amused Burnaby.

Spider suggested a brew up.

The hexi stoves warmed up the general rations – the G rats – and the men ate, spooning the stuff in and dreaming of fillet steak or smoked salmon or steak and kidney pudding. The day wore on and the sun slanted down and the cold stealthily crept in.

By the last of the sun Strike Force was ready to go.

To their disgust, Trampas and Thwackers were detailed off to man the mortar.

"Oh, come on, Tom! Why don't I get a chance of a thwack at them?"

"Because, Thwackers, you are teamed as an oppo with Trampas now. And I want dead-eyed-dick stuff with the mortar when we go in."

Corporal Thwaite saw that he wasn't going to change Burnaby's mind. He grumped around a bit and then started ostentatiously to check the 81 mm mortar. They'd humped the damned thing here, the tube, the base plate, the tripod and the bombs. There was just one mortar and a limited supply of bombs. That was their artillery support. It was a luxury to Strike Force.

Trampas still toted his adapted Bren gun.

"You know, Tom, I'd be more use up with the lads – "

"You and Thwackers on the mortar, Trampas."

"Yeah, well, right … "

Trampas had sustained a light wound during Strike Force's jaunt on the mainland and, although recovered, he was the obvious choice to afford back-up.

That was Burnaby's decision. Not for the first time he reflected on the iniquities of command.

Thwackers was loose because his oppo, Ollie Oliver, had been shot up during Strike Force's attack on Castillos airfield during the same op. Ollie had been a punk rock fanatic.

"Give me E.L.O," Thwackers would say pragmatically. "They have something you can't even begin to understand."

"Get off," Ollie would reply, and manage to contrive an interesting discussion. All that was before Ollie had been shot up by Argentine machine guns.

Taking his place with the General Purpose Machine Gun on this op was the Whizz Kid. He and Q would give sustained covering fire. Burnaby had chosen the Whizz Kid because there was probably nothing to blow up on the feature they were going to assault.

Sawbones, of course, had his usual roving commission. He wouldn't just wait tamely at base. The RAMC doctor would be up there with the lads, ready to give all his skill and devotion to saving their lives if they were hit. Everybody felt a warm and comforting awareness in the presence of Sawbones.

That left two four-man patrols to carry out the assault, plus Barnaby and Andy.

There was probably no profit in trying to be over-clever.

Smyjo would take his patrol in from the right.

Splodge would take his patrol in from the left.

Burnaby and Andy would create mayhem in the centre.

Andy hefted his anti-tank missile launcher.

"The good old Charlie G," he said. "How many tanks they got up there, then, Tom?"

The joke, feeble as it was, cheered Burnaby. The Charlie G might be useful in winkling out enemy from strong points constructed from boulders and turf. No one anticipated any armour being up there.

The two patrols set off, one to the left and the other to the right. Burnaby led Andy straight forward.

Everybody was twitchy about mines.

Burnaby decided not to think about mines.

There was no doubt that he would have liked a few more bodies. Although, in Strike Force, the personnel were not thought of as bodies, mere lumps of flesh and blood to be ordered into action and the dead counted up; each person in Strike Force was an individual, with his own little quirks and funny ways. They meshed superbly as a team because of a number of factors, chief of which was the ruthless training Major Granville had put them through. He'd been selecting and training more recruits when the Falklands mess blew up.

Of course, recruits conjured up the wrong idea.

The men the Major picked out were already superb professional soldiers. He looked for the flair, the dedication, that little extra edge any man of Strike Force must possess. If this thing went on for longer than anyone expected, those new lads would be flown out to join Strike Force.

Burnaby sincerely trusted the whole business would be over in very short order.

But mines ...

The thought wouldn't go away. He had to face it.

He didn't want his leg blown off. He didn't want his inside spilled out. He most certainly did not want to step on one of those bastard devices that popped up trailing a bit of string and blew off your testicles.

The thought of that, and a legless stump to hop about on, appalled him.

Forget it. Get on with the job. And look with the utmost rigorous care at every single step.

Claire Havisham's sister, Anne, who dressed as a frowzy teacher dressed, had vastly surprised him in the matter of legs.

Claire herself, trim, beautiful, long of leg, could be expected to dress and look with a view to knocking a fellow's eyes out. Burnaby conjured up the vision of her strutting on a stage, taking her clothes off to the music, tantalizing, provocative, alluring. She was a vicar's daughter, and stripped to earn a living. Surprising ... And the clerical collar she wore, with its cusp of lipstick, never ceased to stimulate Burnaby.

He'd argued with himself over the best amount of thigh that should be revealed above the stocking top.

That was one invisible benefit accruing from the fashion for ladies to wear tights. The 'Bring Back Stocking Tops' movement was one to which he was passionately attached. These modern lads who saw their girls wearing tights all the time drooled at the sight of stockings and suspender belts.

In the old days *all* the girls wore stockings and suspender belts or corsets. During the war ... Well, they hadn't known they'd had it so good, then.

Nowadays, when a girl wore stockings, and let her man see her in them, she was streets ahead, miles and miles ahead in the allurement business. The naturalness of it appealed strongly. Claire was too beautiful to be real, with a beauty that could easily repel. Anne was so different as to come from another planet.

A boulder ahead appeared to move.

Instantly, Burnaby was flat on the ground, with Andy just to his flank and rear, pressed like a freshly-ironed handkerchief.

Nothing moved.

They waited.

Andy, with the 84mm Carl Gustav, did not stir a muscle. A damned uncomfortable bit of kit was pressing into his gut like a hernia about to explode.

They waited.

Burnaby decided the movement had been a trick of the

vagrant starlight filtered by clouds. Moving with exquisite caution he gave Andy a quick 'stay' motion of his free left hand and then started to ease forward.

The encounter with the sheep had been reported; Burnaby felt convinced there was no one waiting behind that boulder, man, sheep or devil.

The luminous hands of his watch told him there were sixteen minutes left.

Ample time.

In moments like this, creeping forward to the position where an enemy might be waiting with rifle, SMG or grenade to blow off his head, he found himself translated into a different sphere of experience. There was the knowledge that he was scared stiff, and the realization that he just didn't have the time to fool around with being frightened. He had a job to do and he just had to get on with it.

Anything less would swell his chances of being hit and killed.

He wriggled up to the side of the boulder. Andy was positioned off to his flank so that if anyone started anything from the shelter of the boulder, Andy could let fly. The Charlie G rounds were 6½lbs and they'd make an unholy mess of a chap crouching by a rock.

The jaggedy chunk of shadow neared.

Burnaby wiggled cautiously and stopped. He barely breathed. Then, with a little finger-flick, he tossed a pebble. It clicked just off to the side of the darkness.

Nothing.

Well, if anyone *was* there, they were good, damned good.

The blackness lay empty.

Burnaby checked the whoosh of relief, flicked a hand signal to Andy, and pressed on.

He was uncomfortably aware that the Argentinians had excellent night vision devices. Whilst the British forces possessed first generation equipment, in many cases the Argies had second generation kit. The thermal imagers would pick him up, revealing him as a crawling blob in the Argie sights. The cross-hairs would come on, the trigger would be pressed – and Strike Force would be minus one leader.

The realization that he was lying flat abaft a clump of coarse grasses almost surprised him. The mental visualization of that Argie night sight coming on, the trigger being pressed, had been vivid, frighteningly sharp, almost as sharp as the image of Claire's legs. He swallowed bile. Up there the hostiles were probably fast asleep, with a dozy sentry trying to keep warm, confident the hateful British were miles away.

And here he was skulking in a bush.

Highly reprehensible, Burnaby, conduct unbecoming, Burnaby, as Sergeant McArdle might have said.

He checked his watch. Four minutes to the off.

Andy slid up alongside. He found Burnaby's hand and pressed a quick signal.

"Okay?"

"Yes."

Nothing further was necessary.

Burnaby felt more than a fool, he felt a breeze of alarm. What the hell was Andy up to, asking if the CO was okay just before the balloon went up? Had Burnaby himself shown so many signs?

He started off again, rifle cradled, trying to get the dangling Charlie G rounds out of the way. An enormous banging coughing racket erupted from the hill.

He flopped.

A damned great fifty-calibre machine gun was shooting down. Long streaks of fire and the spitting zing of tracers filled the air. The big bullets spattered into the ground, caromed off the rocks, filled everything with the sleet of death.

Tom Burnaby stuck his face into the earth and tried to stop himself from shaking all over.

CHAPTER FIVE

"Come on, Kid! Feed it to the buggers!" Q fairly yelped in his anger, excitement and fervour.

The Whizz Kid opened up with the GMPG from the little sangar they'd built to give themselves some cover.

The bullets scythed up towards that flare of fire where a damned great machine gun was shooting down into the shadows. The noise caromed away across the hillsides. Smoke choked up. And the jimpy laid down a neat pattern all across the Argie machine gun position.

The twinkle of fire up there winked out.

Instantly, the Whizz Kid released pressure and the jimpy gurgled to silence.

Q peered through his own personal and highly expensive piece of night vision kit. In the greenly-blackish glow he could make out the ghostly shapes of rocks and clumps of grasses but not much else. The Argies up there were dug in like it was the Hindenburg Line.

The Whizz Kid had packed essential items for the jimpy, like belts of ammo and his personal bottle, and was moving out. Q grunted, lowered the night sight, and followed.

Over on the mortar position Trampas and Thwackers, with a couple of minutes to go to the off, reacted to that big fifty-calibre showy flare by cutting loose. The mortar bombs, carefully rationed, had to sound and act tonight even bigger than the fifty-calibre. The ranges and targets had been selected as a result of Strike Force's day-long observations. Now, as the mortar bombs sailed away, each with its own distinctive cough of power, Trampas still followed orders. He loosed off in the arranged sequence. Neither he nor Thwackers even considered switching their pattern to begin with the Argie machine gun.

For all they knew, Burnaby and Andy could be in the gunpit right now, dealing with the machine gunners.

From left and right the smashing concussions of the mortar bombs gave comfort to the patrols as they opened up in their turn.

The Argentine positions were drenched in fire.

But a single mortar and a single machine gun firing sustained and half a dozen rifles, plus Trampas's Bren now being operated up front by Taff, could not hope to suppress the entire hill defences. The fifty-calibre Browning opened up again, hammering away, flaring its huge plume of flame into the night.

Burnaby, in the act of getting forward, dropped flat once more as the fifty-calibre bullets cracked and spat about him.

The damned gunner up there had him bracketed all right.

Andy needed no orders or urging.

He got the Charlie G comfortable, holding himself in the lee of the boulder, took careful aim – and let fly.

The 84mm round whistled away, the flame of the discharge a damned great nuisance.

Without waiting to see what happened, Andy rolled over and over away from the spot where he'd loosed off. He came up against a harsh-stemmed grass clump and spread himself as thin as a pancake.

The recoilless rifle's round spattered rock, dirt, grass, in a disintegrating cloud over the machine gun position.

The roar and clatter of fire criss-crossing up and down

the hill took some of the sting away from the explosion, and a mortar bomb crumped almost in time; but, all the same, the bang rang and gonged splendidly.

The fifty-calibre stopped firing.

The Whizz Kid and Q opened up from their new pre-selected position. The mortar ranged into a crest of rocks that had been reported as an Argie sangar. The GMPG loosed off, stopped, and Q and the Whizz Kid packed up and started for another position.

From the flanks, Smyjo's and Splodge's patrols shot into the crest line, keeping the fire taut, moving skilfully into positions that whilst affording cover gave good enfilade lines. No one hung about. Everybody shot, kept low, moved, shot again, kept as flat as possible.

With all this action no one moved an unnecessary inch. Movement gave away positions. But if you stayed in one spot, no matter how good it might appear, you ran the risk of having a concentration of fire called down on your stubborn head. Moderation, combination, coolness – yes, the men of Strike Force knew exactly what they were doing.

Very few of them imagined they had killed even one enemy.

That wasn't the object of this exercise.

Through all the confusion and streaks of fire and the ugly sound of bullets ricocheting past his ears, Burnaby managed to keep up a count of the mortar bombs.

He fancied he might have missed a couple when Andy let fly with his recoilless rifle to take out a winking spot of fire on the hill. But he counted the full initial allowance.

The mortar fell silent.

Andy let rip with his penultimate round, aimed at what looked like a pile of rocks on the crown of the hill. Neither he nor Burnaby waited to see if the rocks remained unmoved or if they exploded. Thev began to crab back, angling down the hill.

At the same time Smyjo and Splodge pulled in their patrols.

The jimpy kept up a covering fire aimed to disconcert the enemy. Now the Whizz Kid was on a free rein and could select targets as they presented themselves. The machine gun jumped about and Q fed the belt through with the meticulous precision it seemed only an RAOC quartermaster officer could contrive.

Under that last furious fire the patrols pulled back. They grouped around in a half-circle angled to the north. They were punctilious about moving into contact, taking full precautions. No member of Strike Force believed in shooting up another member of Strike Force.

The Argentines were not fools. They might not have a wide experience of warfare as waged in Europe or the East, they might only have the experience of chasing and shooting up dissidents, but Burnaby felt it must be pretty obvious to them that they'd only been lightly attacked. They'd been tickled up. They'd be tantalized. But sure as hell – so Burnaby felt – they'd never react other than to sit tight and blast any other attempts on the hill.

When Smyjo showed up, he brought a different reading to the situation.

Smyjo, as the Intelligence Officer of the outfit, knew his way around psychological warfare. He spoke fluent Spanish, which he could approximate into the South American version of that tongue. Now he flopped down in the lee of a bush next to Burnaby.

His tiger-striped face showed a fierce pleasure.

"That wet a few pairs of pants, I'll be bound."

"Still," said Burnaby, carrying on with his own appraisal, "they'll have to be hit again – "

"Possibly not, old boy. It's my guess they imagine they've been under full-scale attack, they've beaten it off with great valour. But – and this is the question – will they hang around to face the next attack?"

Andy said: "Well, we can't hit 'em again until we pick up a resupply. I shot off my last Charlie G brick, the mortar has three left, and the ball ammo is as tight as a virgin's – "

"Quite," said Burnaby.

"I'll be off, then." Q stated this in a matter-of-fact tone that raised no eyebrows and allowed no query. He'd radio back and arrange for the chopper's DZ. The Dropping Zone would have to be manned. It was all go.

"Righto, Q. Give us some warning."

When Q had stomped off in his stolid way, Burnaby produced the map. The Betalamp's glow lit the linen with a weird approximation to the scene through a night sight. He and Smyjo bent over the contours.

Burnaby did think to say: "Smyjo, as the Intelligence Wallah, what odds do you give of the Argies coming down off the hill after us?"

Smyjo passed his stiff forefinger over his upper lip, blinked, and said: "Never."

"We-ell – "

"Or, if they do, we'll hear them like the crowd at Eights Week."

"I see."

Then it was a question of selecting a likely place to have a look for Argies, tickle 'em up and fade.

Sawbones drifted in with a monstrous load of kit he'd humped from their last base.

"I'm always happy when I'm out of work."

"That's the sign of a true artist."

"Is this it?"

"Yeah. Get your head down, Sawbones. We'll be here for the day, now."

On a strict rota basis all of them had the opportunity to sleep. Burnaby sensed that this would be the pattern of the next few days.

Just after midday, the droning chopping of helicopter blades roused him out.

Burnaby squinted up. The weather was going to turn really nasty soon; it held that feeling of cold iron that scraped at the skin, presaging snow. The helicopters circled the rise of the hill and then vanished beyond the crest. The sounds of engines and blades whickered diminuendo to silence.

Smyjo rubbed his hands, beaming.

"Goodoh! Now that's a result worth having."

"Yes."

"The rest of the battalion – at a guess?"

"If not in one lift, then by the time they've finished. We must have scared them good."

The Intelligence Officer was quite right. This was an excellent result. Strike Force had not driven the hostiles off the hill. Instead, the Argies had reinforced the feature. As this area was not among the route possibilities envisaged by the British command, then these troops ought to sit up here out of it, wasted.

Excellent.

They couldn't be down there where the toms and the marines were about to assault the real objectives; not if they were stuck here, pinned by Strike Force.

But, of course, that result wouldn't fully satisfy either Burnaby or Strike Force.

Smyjo voiced the obvious.

"Here," he said, putting an immaculately manicured forefinger on the map which Burnaby had pulled out. "That looks promising. Just because we've got a battalion out on a limb doesn't mean we're finished."

"No – there's the rest of the regiment all lined up and waiting."

As he spoke Burnaby felt himself warming to Smyjo in an unaccustomed way. The big Intelligence Officer seemed to him to appear in a rosy light – most odd.

Then Smyjo said: "You'd better get some shut-eye, Tom."

The guardsman spoke in his usual supercilious way, completely unconscious of his own superiority, unaware how his manner grated on Burnaby.

Instantly, that warm glow vanished. Burnaby felt crud-awful. He drew a breath. Then:

"Right, Smyjo. Will do – "

"That's the style, old boy. Can't have the chief man knocking himself out, now, can we?"

Burnaby rolled off into his hole and huddled down, trying not to think of anything.

But, of course, he thought of Claire and Anne and the car headlights, and of the way that pitiful Skyhawk had disintegrated, and fretted over the poor sod inside who'd never fly over Buenos Aires again ...

CHAPTER SIX

In the next few days Strike Force ran the enemy ragged in their sector. They operated miles behind the front, although there appeared to be no formal front as such. As Burnaby led patrols to strike and fade away only to strike again in an unexpected quarter, he came to believe that most of the Argentine forces were sitting on their backsides in Stanley.

Other groups of special forces were operating nearer to the capital of the islands, striking here, running, striking there, bedevilling the invaders.

The bulk of the enemy forces might still be sitting in Stanley – there were enough outposts and strongpoints to keep Strike Force occupied. The force ranged over the area, quick cut-and-thrust raids never lingering long enough to be caught.

Burnaby decided to stockpile the mortar. Useful though the weapon was, its weight precluded the rapid carriage of required supplies. SSF had to move damned fast when they'd struck so as to hit again from a new quarter. The mortar had proved splendid, dropping its bombs smack on to targets and creating a beautiful unholy row; but it had to go.

Strike Force slimmed down, and many of the fancy weapons carried by the lads when the Major was in field command were discarded.

Q kept up a flow of ammo and grub. A helicopter flew

in whenever Q could lay his sweaty avaricious hands on a loose specimen of the breed. That was not very often; in fact, as Burnaby and Smyjo grouched, it was damned rare. But, somehow, Q kept the force supplied.

On one occasion when Strike Force carried out a hit and run against the Argie position near one of the typical winding inlets of the islands, radio traffic brought a triumphant Q into shore sailing his own boat. He'd borrowed her from the Navy, for Strike Force's rigid raiders were not suitable here. Much chaffing followed that escapade.

Through all this, Q let it be known that he was fed up to the back teeth.

"Oh?"

"Sure. When do I go on another little picnic as they used to say?"

Smyjo brushed his forefinger over his upper lip. Burnaby looked the other way.

Andy said: "We're stocked up with everything, Tom. Right now. Why don't Q – ?"

"Sure," said Burnaby, still not looking at Smyjo. "We believe there's an Argie post just right for you, Q. Tonight."

Lieutenant Charlie Mainwaring beamed.

An odd little incident occurred on that op.

Burnaby, Smyjo and Andy, angling around the locus of the firefight, stumbled upon a slit trench – an affair a little more grand than a foxhole or scrape, not as impressive as a real dugout – which, although probably half-filled with cold water, was occupied by two terrified Argentinian soldiers.

They were jabbering away to each other, and one was interrupting what he was saying to scream in a most distressing way.

"What the hell – ?" said Andy.

Smyjo interpreted.

"One of 'em's had his foot blown off. We're in the middle of a minefield here."

The ice-cold skeletal hand that crawled down Burnaby's spine might have been a figment of his imagination. It was real enough to him. He felt the shock of it go through him like an icicle.

"Mines?" said Andy, lying with his nose in the ground.

He drew his bayonet and prepared to find a safe way back. The Brits had been divinely lucky they had not trodden on a mine so far. Away to their left the rattle of machine guns and the crashing crump of Charlie G rounds announced the brisk little fight was nearing its climax.

Smyjo said: "Those two are too scared to do anything." He began to help Andy to search for the safe way back. Then he said, with a strange lightness of tone: "They blew themselves up getting there to man this outpost. The silly buggers don't even know where their own mines are!"

In a voice too sharp, yet still modulated to carry to his comrades' ears and not those of the caterwauling Argies, Burnaby said: "One of 'em has lost a foot? Is that all?"

"Yes, apart from yelling for help."

"Still," said Andy, calmly, in perfect control. He began to work on the mine less than six inches from Smyjo's foot. Smyjo glanced around, saw what the sergeant-major was doing, and stilled.

Burnaby said: "He'll die from loss of blood unless he's treated."

Tightly, watching Andy, Smyjo said: "Let his pal carry him out, then."

The normal reaction of the ordinary soldier, in the midst of a battle and subject to all the shocks and fears of imminent death, if he learned that his enemy had blown himself up on his own mine would be to laugh his head off and go off whistling. That was the ordinary sensible natural – however incomprehensible to the non-soldier – reaction.

Burnaby knew he was wrong.

Burnaby knew he shouldn't have done it.

All the same, Tom Burnaby was rather up to here in deaths and killings and maimings. He was wrong; but he did it all the same.

"Shout across to them Smyjo. Tell them help is coming."

That Smyjo failed to grasp what was in Burnaby's mind did not surprise him.

Smyjo said: "That won't keep them quiet for long." He shouted across in Spanish, head low, mouth upturned in such a way as to convey the impression of a cynical grin. That, Burnaby recognized, was altogether unfair on the gallant guardsman.

Andy saw at once.

"I'll come, Tom, as well. You – "

"No, Andy."

Somebody higher up let rip with a belting string of fifty-calibre rounds. The Argies seemed to possess hundreds of the Yank Browning machine guns, and they used them like garden hoses. The three Brits stuck their heads and bottoms down and tried to worm into the frosty ground.

When the fire eased up, Andy said: "Tom – you'll get your fool head blown off for no reason – "

"Maybe, Andy. You and Smyjo better try and find Smartie. If he's trodden on a mine – "

"He's like a bad penny."

"I trust so. Right, I'm off."

Smyjo still didn't believe.

"What the hell, Tom!"

"He'll bleed to death with a foot blown off. His pal sounds as though he's scared stiff. It's very simple."

The mine Andy cleared away turned out to be an Italian SB33 anti-personnel plastic job. Strike Force were familiar with a large and varied assortment of mines, and detested the lot, and Intelligence had warned them that the Argentines had Italian mines. They had others, also, no doubt.

There was no point hanging about. Flashes and explosions lit the night. The noise ebbed and flowed with the nuances of the breeze. The op for tonight had not included this; but Burnaby went ahead.

Moving with caution, watching and prodding for the nasty little three-inch diameter plastic turds of death, he approached the slit trench.

He disposed of two more – and that took time, time! – put his head down by the lip of uppermost rock and babbled the words Smyjo used. A voice quavered weakly.

"*Qué?*"

Oh, hell! said Burnaby to himself and rolled over into the trench. It was only a bit of a scrape, after all, the front parapet heightened by rocks. He grabbed the first well-wrapped figure and shook him and stared straight into the man's frightened face. He showed his teeth.

"Shut up, you idiot!"

The fellow was like a bag of flour in his fists.

The other one lay as sprawled as possible in that tiny place, holding on to the bottom of his leg. At least they'd managed to get some sort of bandage around the stump.

Burnaby bent, grabbed the wounded man and started to hoist him out. The other one went mad, clawing at the Briton, trying to drag him back. Burnaby clipped him – not too hard – and then, by gestures, made him help in getting his comrade out of the trench.

It was a process that Burnaby had no wish to remember. Between them, Argentine and Briton half-carried, half-dragged the wounded man through the minefield and clear of its farther edge. There had been a single strand of barbed wire on the inner side to demarcate the field; most of that was missing.

Andy said: "Now what?"

Burnaby felt as though his insides were ballooning up. He wasn't going to be sick. No, sir! But he felt – odd.

"Just send 'em off back to their buddies."

"Right."

Andy, with the true British gift of languages made signs, whispered with fierceness, and only just refrained from kicking bottoms as he sent the two Argies back to their comrades. They were clearly dazed. Burnaby hoped they'd make it. The one with the foot missing looked pretty awful.

The odd thing was that in all the confusion as he'd dropped into their trench and sorted them out he hadn't thought at all. Really and truly, as he rolled into their trench, he should have been trying to kill them rather than save their lives. That they ought to have been trying to kill him, and weren't, didn't seem unusual either.

Odd.

He became aware that the machine gun fire was slackening. Return fire came in short bursts.

Time to depart.

Smyjo had found Smart, who had been detained in a hole by a couple of Argies.

When Smart and Smyjo rejoined, the two departing Argies chose that moment to clamber over a little tussocky hillock to get to their own lines beyond.

"Two of 'em – " yelped Smart and lifted his rifle.

Burnaby froze.

The folly of his own actions now became crystal clear.

He had a personal interest in those two Argies. Yet how could he knock down Smart's rifle? What possible explanation could he offer for not carrying out his duty?

With a mouth that seemed lined with dust, he said:

"Hold your fire, Smartie, old lad. Poor sods. They can't do us any more harm."

Smart lowered his SLR.

He cocked an eye at Burnaby, started to say: "You sound – " stopped, and was silent. He couldn't remember when Tom Burnaby had ever called him old lad before.

Q joined them, looking pleased with himself. He was carrying an expensive-looking piece of night-sight kit, and he even had his handkerchief out, polishing it up.

"I reckon they'd just unpacked this from the crate. Fresh delivered from the U.S.A. May not be as good as some of our latest, but it's a fine example."

"Sure," said Burnaby, feeling the broken tension with overwhelming relief. "And you can carry it, Q."

"Pleased to, pleased to."

They went down off the little hill, collected Strike Force and set off for the location of the new base. As they hacked along, Burnaby knew again that he should not have done what he had done. He had imperilled his own life, the chances of success, he'd done it all wrong.

If he had it to do again, he knew damn well he'd do just the same.

The Argie who'd had his foot blown off looked to be in his mid twenties, with rank markings. His comrade could only have been seventeen or eighteen, a miserable, frightened conscript. Well, there were lads of seventeen with the British paratroops, nothing marvellous about that. Just that youth made killing that much more beastly. No, he'd do the same wrong actions all over again, just as he had with Miss Claire and Miss Anne Havisham.

The sight of Claire's smashed-up face in the hard glare of the headlights. The flash of Anne's remarkable underclothes. Well, maybe, just maybe, he hadn't done *everything* wrong.

CHAPTER SEVEN

The idea of Argentine mines bothered Burnaby.

Intelligence had suggested they were likely to encounter Italian mines. This they had done.

But Spider, in his semi-flippant way, remarked that he'd had to deal with an Israeli Number Four anti-personnel box mine. The bastard thing had been fitted with a trip wire and used as a booby trap. A big Yank anti-tank M1 mine dating from World War Two had been wired in.

"Nasty, boy-oh," said Taff, polishing up his bayonet. "The sappers can't detect these plastic horrors with their vacuum cleaners, see."

No one minded Taff and his funny ways.

Strike Force were not indulging in a day off from the campaign. They worked on their weapons in base camp, sent out patrols, tried to rest up. They were waiting for Q and his supply party to return with more ammo and grub.

Their task here, unlike that of the special forces around Stanley and on the route towards the capital, was not to take and hold ground, or at least to deny it to the enemy. Their task was to make nuisances of themselves, to draw in extra enemy reinforcements, and to force the Argentine commander to expend men and resources on a sector which would be by-passed.

That was the plan.

Smyjo sat with his back against his pack, working on his notebook, his pencil every now and then stroking across his upper lip. He had said nothing at all to Burnaby about the latter's foolish escapade with the two enemy soldiers.

Now he looked up and stared at Burnaby.

"In my view, Tom, we've done enough here to make the Argies hate us so much they'll task a group to Take Steps."

"Oh?"

"Too right. They'll come after us."

"Great!" said Spider. "We'll hide in a hole and blow 'em away when they wander past."

"Q.E.D." Lawless, Spider's oppo, spoke with sarcasm.

"But Spider's right," went on Smyjo. "The Argies won't send idiots after us. They'll use special forces – Buzo Tactico or some group like that. They're tough."

"We've tangled with them before," pointed out Burnaby.

"Sure."

"So, we do like Spider says."

"Oh, yes." Smyjo flipped his notebook cover. "We'll slap them down, old boy."

"One thing." Burnaby glanced around the camp. From this angle he could see the stacks of rocks, the spread ponchos, the weapons. From only a few metres above the position was invisible.

"Yes, old boy?"

"We don't want them to find us when we're low on ammo. That means we go out and find them when we're loaded and fully kitted up."

"Too right!"

Radio traffic on the Argentine frequencies was monitored. Smyjo did his best to make sense of it all, but there was little to be gained. When the hostiles set out they'd do it by the book.

The fact that a number of Argentine officers had gone through British training courses would add a certain piquancy to the forthcoming situation.

Pundits might claim that Falklands weather held to a remarkably even curve through the seasons of the year. Burnaby could sense the onset of winter. The wind held a keener bite, the air a more frosty tang. If this thing wasn't settled soon, then the Brits might find themselves facing the dismal prospect of a winter out in the open.

That might prove more costly than anyone cared to envisage.

Get the job done, march into Stanley, liberate the people from their foreign aggressors – and then go home.

That was the style!

The news that 2 Para had taken Goose Green was received with great relief. At last events were moving. Hammer picked up the signals on the big radio and relayed them to the others waiting expectantly.

"That's the southern flank," said Smyjo, beaming.

"We could have done without the casualties, though," pointed out Splodge. "Particularly the CO." He looked upset. "Bloody business." He was not in a communicative mood for a time after that.

Major Granville when selecting personnel for Strike Force had not unnaturally gone to the Parachute Regiment for men of the highest quality. The death of men from 2 Para together with their Commanding Officer was a matter of great consequence and was received in Strike Force with dismay. They had seen their own comrades killed in this campaign, had seen them wounded. Everyone understood that before that triumphal march into Stanley there were going to be more deaths.

Burnaby had had death on his mind back in England when he'd gone down to Bovington for an interview. He did not particularly want the offered job, interesting though it would undeniably be. He'd been accepted into Strike Force, despite not being Granville's first choice, and revelled in the opportunities he could see coming up.

Death had struck calmly and horribly.

A young signalman had fallen from the side of a lorry, slap into the track of a Chieftain.

Before the driver could do anything to avert the tragedy the tank's track had rolled over the youngster. Burnaby had helped scrape him up. That memory, pungent, bitter and altogether ghastly, remained with him.

He had not had a lot of leave since those sneaked weekends to try to see Claire; now he grabbed the chance to go up to London. He wanted to see Sheila Crumley.

She might well know what was going on.

As far as Burnaby understood the mechanics of the business lurking behind the strippers' jobs, the girls went on the circuit. They performed their act in one club and then packed up, raced down the street to the next, and the next.

Sheila had, through the interest of one owner, aspired to being the star of the show, with her own dressing-room. The ex-broom cupboard afforded her enough space to stretch out her long legs, to hang her wardrobe, to find a place for the basket that was home to her pekinese – Lord Scaramouche – and just leave enough room for a chair in which her guests might crouch. Burnaby, in civvies, duly crouched. He kept well away from Lord Scaramouche. He did not wish to lose a sizeable chunk of flesh from either one of his own legs.

Ms Crumley was in the most furious of tempers, sullen moodiness alternating with gusts of passionate anger.

The inevitable bottle of Pernod sat on her tiny dressing table, and the glass looked well-used.

"Out," she said. "Out, like an old boot!"

Diplomatically, Burnaby nodded, listened, agreed from time to time and wondered when he could interrupt the flood of invective to introduce the topic of Claire Havisham.

"That Max," she ranted on. "He's a nothing, a bit-part in a farce. When I think what I've done for him ... " She slopped Pernod, drank, didn't offer any of the stuff to Burnaby, for which he was grateful.

The fullness of Sheila's figure complemented her round, saucy face, her bright brown eyes, her high colour. At the moment she was a redhead. Had she wished to be a blonde or a brunette, wigs crowned the bald plastic skulls to hand. No doubt being a redhead exactly suited her tempestuous mood.

Her own, her very own hair, mousey and thin, normally was crammed into a silky cap.

"The way that Max treats me ... I'm an artiste. The bastard just grins when I explain. I'm going to support the Strippers' Action Group." She drank some more, tilting her head back, letting the rot-gut flow. "I should say Strip-tease Artistes' group. The AGM of Equity was where it was at."

"Oh?"

"Sure, sure. We're not treated as proper professional entertainers. And we are! We're exploited, that's what Candy told me, and she should know. We work for peanuts. If we were organised, less isolated, that's what Candy says."

Burnaby wasn't the slightest bit interested in Candy.

"You get a young kid, down the boozer on the local corner, not top class, just beginning. She does three solid hours of dancing, topless dancing, mind you – well, Tom? How much is that paid?"

"No idea."

"Eight to ten quid, that's what. For three hours of swinging it about. It's not right, it's not right."

"Well," said Burnaby, very carefully. "A lot of blokes don't go into pubs to see young kids flaunting their figures, you know." He smiled. "There is the beer."

He hadn't been anywhere near careful enough.

Ms Crumley's ensuing explosion brought Lord Scaramouche growling from his basket. Sheila raved at him, waving her arms about, her eyes seeming to blaze sparks. She threw the glass at him and the dregs of Pernod splattered the wardrobe. She screamed.

"Just like men! That's all you think of! Let me tell you, any girl's got more go in her little finger than any man's got in his whatsit! You're a fine one to talk, gawping after the girls – leching about after Claire! Let me tell you – "

Burnaby stood up, knocking over a box of trinkets in the process.

"Sheila – I respect your work. If Max is throwing you out, then, of course, you have every right to protest." He tried to be cunning. "I was only pointing out that this little kid doing her topless go-go stuff you mentioned, and you – why, there's a world of difference, isn't there?"

That took her aback. She pondered, reaching for the bottle. Taking his advantage, Burnaby said: "Claire? Have you seen her lately, Sheila?"

She waved the bottle at him. Liquid sloshed over her lace chemise. The scent of her perfume stifled him in the cubicle-like dressing-room.

"No. I heard she was making a stag film."

Burnaby knew about that. He had taken himself off when his investigation revealed Claire about to take her clothes off before the video cameras. He'd gone back to the house in its leafy lane in the country to find the place deserted. But, if Sheila knew that, she might know more – might know who was making this dismal film and where he might contact them.

"Sheila! Look – do you know who's making this film? Where can I find them?"

She glanced down at herself, the Pernod bottle tilted uncaringly. The liquid spread across the lace chemise.

"Huh?"

"This film, Sheila. Claire – "

"I don't know. How the hell should I know? Bunch of creeps. Like Max, I shouldn't wonder."

Burnaby sat tight, seething, hoping that this wasn't another dead end.

She put down the bottle and miraculously it remained upright. She started to pull the chemise away from her body, grimacing, and then crossed her arms, gripped the hem and hauled. Even then, she hauled with great care. That lace not only tore easily – it cost a fair proportion of a stripper's salary.

Burnaby ducked.

The cubicle called a dressing-room allowed a certain amount of movement. Burnaby felt his chair squeezed against the wall as Sheila threw the chemise on top of a discarded copy of the *Sun*. She stretched. The room was drenchingly hot. Then she picked up a fluffy mauve towel and clucked as it refused to remove the sticky drink from her skin.

Burnaby could barely stand up to say goodbye.

"You going, then, Tom? You know what I said about this nonsense with you and Claire." There was a good deal of her to wash clean in the miniscule sink. "Now Max has booted me out, the rotten perv, you and me could – "

"I'll be – ah – out of the country for a month or so."

"Really? Benidorm? Ibiza? Why don't you take me along? I'm free right now."

"It's not a holiday – "

She half turned, swingingly, to regard him from over the towel.

"Yeah, you never did say what you do for a living.

"Businessman. And I must fly – "

She laughed. "You're out of this world, Tom. You're so out of date it's funny."

She was quite right, of course.

He looked at her as she rubbed the towel down herself. In a flash of insight he saw the hurt in her, the feelings of despair and abandonment. For all her tough sophisticated act, the modern girl with a career and a finger up to all men, she was as vulnerable as anybody else.

Impulsively he took the two steps that were all that were necessary to reach her.

For a single instant an expression flared in her face. He bent and kissed her – lightly – on the lips.

Before she could drop the towel and grab him, he turned away, opened the door.

"Goodbye. Your career will be okay, Sheila."

"You – "

Stuck here in a sodden scrape on a hillside in the Falklands, without a pint of Mackesons within God knew how many thousand miles, he wondered just how many of the lads in Strike Force would have gone away and closed the door.

Sheila was overpoweringly luscious. That was the trouble as far as Burnaby was concerned. He had got over the desire to have sex with every woman he met, no matter what they looked like. It wasn't that he was picky, just that he'd come to terms with his own sexuality and was determined to make his life hold a proper balance. He was not at all sure that Claire Havisham was right for him. She was vastly experienced, that seemed perfectly obvious. He didn't know if he loved her or not. She bothered him.

But whilst Claire existed there could not be a Sheila in his life.

CHAPTER EIGHT

"They told me when I joined up," said Spider, using his spoon to gobble mouthfuls between phrases, "never volunteer for anything."

"A sound principle – for some," observed his oppo, Lawless.

Burnaby looked on these two with bright affection. Spider and Lawless. On these two he would rely with that fraction of extra repect accorded Andy and one or two others. That was human nature, to select and order, to arrange.

"If I understand you two correctly – " he began.

"We two idiots," said Spider. "We two gallant lads who are off our chumps."

"Amen," said Lawless.

Trampas spoke belligerently.

"You going to stop me getting stuck in again this time, Tom?"

Thwackers, teamed with Trampas, looked on eagerly.

Andy cleared his throat, but remained silent.

Burnaby said: "It'll take four blokes to make it look right. A four-man patrol will fit in with what the Argies are expecting." He looked around the men, squatting in their circle, their faces tiger-striped, their eyes and teeth bright, their rifles and SMG's casually angled up as though ready for action. "All right. Spider, Lawless, Trampas, Thwackers – you're the Low Party."

"And we," said Smyjo with great venom, "will descend on the hostiles from a great height."

Burnaby, recollecting Sergeant McArdle's little sayings, did not smile, but the moment warmed.

"There's one problem, though," pointed out Andy.

"Sure there is," broke in Spider.

Lawless twitched at his rifle.

"Yeah. But they're probably lousy shots."

"Ah, no ... " Smyjo did not brush his forefinger over his upper lip. He was serious. "These johnnies are special forces. They can shoot straight."

At that moment the wind scoured across the hillside, stirring the grasses, blowing chill and unpleasantly.

The fact that the enemy were not little conscripts and could shoot straight was not in itself likely to deter the men of Strike Force. A certain frisson was building. They were going up against men who had been trained to be like they were themselves. They'd done this before, and suffered casualties, and won through.

This time would not be any different. Would it?

"Get some kip," advised Burnaby. "Reveille oh five hundred.

Strike Force were going to operate in the daytime, abandoning the concealing cloak of darkness. Many of the advantages of night-time operations were lost, anyway, because of the good night-vision equipment possessed by the enemy. Everybody had a try at the kit Q had brought back from his share of the previous action, and they all knew what they were up against in that department.

"One thing," Burnaby said before he rolled into his sleeping bag, "we won't have any damned mines to worry about."

"Fank Gawd."

Whoever said that voiced all their sentiments.

Just before he dozed off Burnaby found himself

wondering why on earth men had to kip down in sleeping bags in a damp hole in the ground on an island not noted for ease of living, when they could be snuggling up to soft round forms under white sheets in snug beds in England.

Or Argentina, come to that.

The whole business was a madness. Some of the lads actively enjoyed roughing it, sleeping in the open, tangling with men they had been given permission to kill.

Like any of them, Burnaby would do his share.

He couldn't say he enjoyed it.

Take that Sheila, for instance. He had not been able to take advantage of her offer. But now, down here in the Falklands – well, Goddammit! At least he'd have had one more happy memory to go over and over again and warm himself on.

He did not particularly want to think of Claire as he had seen her, all bruised and dazed, stumbling in the headlights' glare.

There was a mystery about Claire – well, at that time he had felt convinced there was a mystery about Claire – which he was unable to solve. He'd decided that her sister Anne might give him a lead. She had been far less than co-operative when they'd last met so that he could only hope she would prove more helpful this time.

The decision actually to go back to the vicarage where the sisters lived with their father came to him not effortlessly, but without too much mental wrestling. Claire usually only stayed at the vicarage when she was down from town, her work, which her father believed to be as a high-powered personal assistant in the City, detaining her for much of the time. Anne lived there because the place was her home. She taught school for her living, and already Burnaby suspected she was a very good schoolmarm indeed.

The sleeping bag cocooned him. He felt warm and lazy – remarkable feelings in his situation. He wondered why it was that people always seemed to be able to find other people to dislike. Hatred between men and men, women and women, seemed to be a natural attribute to humankind. Most odd. That flash of fellow feeling for Smyjo he'd experienced, before the natural arrogance of the woodentop had ruined it – wasn't that how it ought to be?

Of course, if a terrorist or a gangster or, here, an Argentinian, tried to kill him he'd have to stop that. If the silly sod got himself killed in the process then that was his own stupid fault.

Anne was in the garden when he called. She wore a voluminous flowing dress, all yellow flowers and brown leaves on a drab background – damned ugly.

The cut roses glowed against that incongruous dress. Her straw hat, shielding her face against the brilliant sunshine, had ragged edges. She held the secateurs dangerously.

He apologized for intruding.

She recognized him from their previous encounter by the swimming pool.

"I have nothing to say to you. Will you please leave."

The scent of roses caught at Burnaby. He delighted in the perfumes of flowers.

He tried to make a disarming gesture, a warm smile, be ingenuous.

"You have a lovely garden here, Miss Havisham – "

"I am Miss Anne Havisham. My sister is Miss Havisham."

"Ah – of course. Silly of me."

"No. The fashion is to ignore little things like that these days. Now, if you will excuse me – "

"Look, Miss Anne – you seem to think I want to harm Claire. That's completely wrong. I want to help her. I think she's in trouble, somehow, and –

"There is nothing you can do."

Despite her words, she did not move away. The roses against her dress moved with her breathing. She held the secateurs as though they were a weapon to fend him off.

"So there *is* something wrong?"

"Claire told me about you – "

"But that was a complete misunderstanding!"

"She said you were kind to her when she was insulted in a public house. Afterwards you tried to rape her."

"No! Look here. What can I say – do I look the kind of man to go around raping people?"

Now she licked her lips. The straw hat made any reading of her expression difficult. A tilt of her head suddenly brought a liquid gleam into her eyes, a flash that vanished as suddenly as it appeared.

"I – I would not know ... "

"If you'd just let me tell you what happened, explain. Good Lord! It's not very complicated."

A bee buzzed past, fat and pollen-clogged. The warmth of the day filled the air with pleasure. She held the roses to her; but the secateurs dangled until they rested limply against her side. Her hands were white, white and shapely and bearing little traces of the garden dirt. She wore no shoes or stockings.

Burnaby felt a tiny shock. Her toenails were painted a deep shining crimson.

"Well – I'm not sure – "

"Just give me a chance to explain."

She took a breath. "Very well. But, I warn you – "

"Then we can discuss how we can help Claire."

She turned towards the house. Burnaby started to follow, and felt a hand on his shoulder and a voice – hardly Anne's voice, for it was deep and gruff – said: "Oh four fifty-five, Tom. Reveille."

Instantly, Burnaby sat up, knowing where he was and

what was laid on for the day.

"Spider's just brewing up."

Burnaby rubbed his hair.

"You had some sleep, Andy?"

"Yes."

"H'm. I don't want you dozing off in the middle of a fire fight."

The camp stirred to activity. Burnaby rolled out and stood up.

There was a bitter cut to the wind. The place they'd set up gave some shelter; but not for the first time Burnaby realised how much he missed the presence of trees. That had surprised him at the beginning. He'd always liked trees and flowers, but he'd never regarded himself as a tweedy nature-lover. But a few oaks, or poplars, some willows too – then he grimaced. They'd all be bending away from the eternal wind, trying to stop their roots from being dragged out of the peaty soil. What a place!

In these circumstances the little hexi stoves were a Godsend. Hot food inside a fellow made a deal of difference to his outlook on life.

Preparations necessary were only those few last-minute checks. Everything had been readied overnight.

Burnaby felt a tiny damp sting on his cheek, and put his hand up in automatic reflex.

Andy looked up.

"Spot of snow, Tom?"

"Looks like it. Confound it!"

"Oh, I don't know. They won't see us too clearly when we jump 'em."

"That's true. But we won't see them as easily, either."

"If it gets down my neck – that's when I get annoyed."

They both smiled. They could recall that time in Norway when Andy had tumbled headlong down a long snow slope, and come up coated with the stuff, spluttering, and swearing he was off winter for life. That training could harden the lads was undeniable. They just took bad weather as it came. But in all honesty you couldn't claim they were enamoured of it.

The plan was simple, as most of the best plans were. Everyone understood what was to happen and what each person was to do.

The Argentines had sent out a special forces patrol to catch Strike Force. Strike Force were going to turn the tables, play cat and mouse, use the hostiles' intentions as a weapon against them.

The single most worrying feature about the whole business for Burnaby was the role of Low Party. Spider, Lawless, Trampas and Thwackers were not exactly bait in a trap; but what they were going to do bore perilously close to that idea. Burnaby knew he was a fool to fret. The plan had been agreed, the different posts were filled. Low Party would be all right.

They bloody well had to be.

When they set out, humped under essentials-only burdens, moving along in single file abaft Burnaby in the lead, a few clammy flakes of snow whipped past in the wind.

The temperature was down. If it was going to start snowing then conditions were just about perfect.

Bulky, powerful men, warmly clothed, well-armed, they hacked along the angles of the hills, circling the slopes, making sure they did not break a skyline crest. When the time was right they'd let the Argies know they were around.

The coarse grasses stretched away on every side, rustling uneasily. The air held an icy tang. They marched stolidly on, alert, watchful, ready for the sudden whirr of helicopter blades, the whining purring of a Pucara, or – even and remotely so – the whip and crack of a sniper's bullet.

The daylight, such as it was when it crawled furtively

up out of the banks of overcast, served only to give depth and perspective to the bleak and desolate nature of this place.

Yet people lived here. They kept sheep. They had their own lives in their stations, and a social whirl when they could get to Stanley. They were British. Silly to think they'd want to be involved with the ghastly carryings-on of Argentina. And Strike Force laboured on to take out one little group of hostile special forces who no doubt considered themselves the finest, with a Galtieri-given mission to exterminate the British and dominate all the people of the islands.

CHAPTER NINE

Low Party slogged through a shallow valley between low and rounded hills.

Spider felt as though tiny spiders were running up and down his backbone. This was like standing up among the clay pipes in an old-time shooting gallery. He'd always liked going to the fair at Whitsun weekend. He'd never bothered much with the stupid games that just rooked you of your pennies. And the dodgems and the wheels and the whirlers and spinners were all right if you could keep your supper down. No – he'd liked the shooting gallery.

He'd won enough teddy bears and dolls and knick-knacks to load his bedroom shelves. He gave them away, mostly, towards the end.

He marched on, his Light Support Weapon cocked and angled, ready to go.

Lawless, carrying his Personal Weapon as a poacher or a gamekeeper would, followed. He did not feel tiny spiders up and down his backbone; he did feel the pressure of eyes watching his every movement.

Like them all, he continually scanned the low horizon, trying to spot the first movement up there. The first thing they'd know if they were ambushed would be the crack of a bullet between the eyes.

"Just how good are these bleeding Argie special forces?" grumbled Trampas.

"Depends who they are," Thwackers told him. "Could be marines, commandos, Navy torture squads, blokes like ourselves – just depends."

"You mean we're Navy torture squads, Thwackers?" Spider's quip did not go down well with the others.

They stalked on, senses tuned, ready to break, dive flat and open fire.

Just bleeding walking targets, said Spider to himself, and stalked on, feeling more and more savage.

Spider, like his three companions, knew that the situation was not as clear-cut as it seemed. They were not just perambulating along on their own waiting to be shot at. Oh, no. The rest of the lads were up there, eyes like hawks, positioned to blow away the first sign of Argie interference.

"Talk about the Divis," he said to himself. What they were up to down here in the Falklands was supposed to be real soldiering, as opposed to the mess in Northern Ireland. There was bound to be a feeling among the troops that a real old-fashioned battle with your enemies in front and permission to shoot with intent had just got to be better than waiting to be blown up or sniped with sod all to do in return.

Spider hunched his right shoulder a trifle, then made himself relax. The flicks and flacks of snow couldn't decide if they should blow up into a real storm or go away and let the sun shine. The wind persisted, a chill nasty blast; but Spider kept his eyes swivelling, checking out the landscape, turning his head, ignoring the cold.

The presence of old Lawless at his back was a great comfort – hell, great comfort? Lawless was a rip-roaring, essential, wonderful, absolutely irreplaceable part of Spider's life now. Mind you, they could slang each other rotten when they felt like it. But if an Argie crept up to the slope of a hill – say that hill there – Lawless would, in Spider's book, be the first bloke to spot the blighter.

After that it would be a split-second affair between the two as to the fastest draw and the straightest shoot.

Good old Trampas was moaning again. Spider smiled to himself. If there wasn't a genuine groaning complaint around, Trampas could manufacture one with great aplomb. Now they walked along this valley and waited for bullets to scythe down and cut them to pieces –

Spider told himself to shut up.

Tom knew what he was doing. And that maniac Smyjo wouldn't let them down. They hacked on, the white rinds of their eyes the brightest thing about them.

One of the tragedies of Strike Force had affected Trampas more than the others, for it had been his oppo Jock who had been tortured to death over there on the mainland. Thought of that braced a man up. Some of the Argies were just miserable conscripts; some were dedicated killers. All of them, from what could be ascertained, had jumped for joy when Argentina invaded and forcibly took over the Falkland Islands.

A thought hit Spider. It did not seem possible. In fact, it was impossible. But – but, just suppose? Just suppose the Argentine special forces unit out here now was the same one they'd tangled with over on the mainland!

The hideous creature calling itself Captain Alvilas had been taken off wounded. So he couldn't be commanding this unit. But – just suppose they were the same outfit ...

Thwackers called softly from the rear: "Break for ten."

They were in a shallow depression, almost a dell, amongst the grasses, with rather less of the ubiquitous rocks scattered around. They did not intend to hang around for long. Thwackers must have something cooking in that long head of his.

Spider squatted, LSW slanted up between his knees.

"Hey, suppose this lot we're chasing – "

"This lot chasing us, you mean, Spider?" asked Lawless.

"They might be chasing you, chum; I'm chasing them!"

"Right."

"Well, suppose they're the same lot we duffed up over on the mainland?"

A little silence followed, then.

Lawless said seriously: "So what if they are? They're just Argies. We know they're supposed to be something special. But it makes no difference – does it?"

"Not to me," said Trampas. He'd put out of his mind the horrendous thoughts of Jock. He did not wish to have them brutally thrust back into his head; sleep was precious.

Strike Force had taken knocks in this campaign.

Trampas had lost his oppo. Thwackers' oppo, Ollie Oliver, had been wounded. Now the survivors were teamed together.

"We-ell," said Thwackers. "I wouldn't mind putting a few into those bastards who shot Ollie up."

Trampas didn't want to hear this.

He stood up cautiously and moved off a space. The others thought he wanted to relieve himself – and that was true in a way they hadn't grasped. The wind whistled and the clouds pressed down. Flakes of snow swirled and vanished. The light was like that in an aquarium, shifting and treacherous. Trampas breathed deeply, automatically looking around the skyline, trying to let any movement up there flow naturally into the corners of his eyes.

Spider looked after Trampas and shook his head.

"I wish the idiot would get Jock off his chest."

"Maybe when this little lot's over. One thing – it certainly hyped Trampas up. I thought that knock he took might have blotted him otherwise."

"Nah," pointed out Thwackers. "He's the same as all of us."

On this profound philosophical thought Trampas came back and the patrol shook itself out to finish the tramp through this particular valley.

They reached to within a hundred metres of the far end when, through the eternal soughing of a wind, a chop-chopping flutter of sound reached them.

In normal circumstances they would have dived for the cover of the nearest clump of thicker grasses, or dropped prone and lain rigidly still.

In these unusual circumstances they readied themselves to act like loons.

The helicopter swung up abruptly over the flank of the hill to their front right.

She was a Hughes 500M Defender, a stubby, round-nosed little beast, probably one of the batch licence-made in Argentina. She came whirring along low over the ground towards the four-man patrol.

Instantly they started to do foolish things.

Spider jumped up and down and then ran like a headless chicken away to his left. Lawless copied him and charged off back the way he'd come. Trampas, after a belligerently hostile look up, started to run towards the slope to his right, turned away from the low-flying helo. Thwackers ran around in a complete circle, and then angled back, away from Trampas but still over to the right.

They did all these things in mere heartbeats.

Before the chopper had time to react to their antics they were taking genuine evasive actions.

A glance flung over his shoulder told Spider that he'd picked the line the chopper was following. She'd vaulted over the slope of the hill to his front right, and was now steering straight for him. Immediately he changed his direction to angle even farther to his right, swinging almost at ninety degrees to the chopper.

The others seemed simply to vanish into the ground.

Spider hoped the helicopter pilot would make the reasonable assumption that the British soldier below him, shatteringly surprised by the chopper's appearance, had panicked. Waiting until he knew he could wait no longer, Spider stopped short, turned around, and ran like a sprinter in the opposite direction.

It had to bloody well be him, of course! He had to be the one the chopper lined up on!

The Hughes Defender might only be the basic model, without later refinements, but she still carried a formidable armament. The anti-armour missiles she was probably carrying would not do him much harm. But she'd have a couple of machine guns, possibly a cannon, and these could shred him to a pulp. The tadpole shape of the chopper turned to follow his original run, her blades glinting. When Spider changed direction the chopper pilot made instant corrections to his course. He was a good pilot. But the gunner had allowed deflection for Spider's initial run.

Bullets started to cut up the ground, sending gouts of dark earth high into the air.

The rattle and bang sounded alarmingly loud. Spider was not likely to be too discomfited by the sheer volume of noise, however unwholesome it might be. He ran full tilt, dived, found a crevice abaft a clump of the heavy grasses, and disappeared.

The gunner really murdered the area of the Falklands where he'd expected the British soldier to be.

By the time the helicopter had tilted and swung around to bring her on line, there was no sign below of any life at all.

The Britons lay motionless.

The chopper swung wide, taking more time than Spider thought necessary to complete her half-circle and clip-clop back. Cunning bastard! Spider reflected to himself that these Argie pilots knew their business. This one had decided that a seemingly slow return might induce the soldier below to make a fresh run for it.

He was disappointed.

Trampas fingered the trigger of his weapon and refrained from sending a burst up into that fat tadpole shape.

The chopper searched backwards and forwards. Wearing camouflage clothing, however inefficient in this particular Falklands scenery, and using full anti-surveillance techniques, the Brits escaped detection. The light was bad, anyway, and no doubt the pilot was more concerned in reporting his observations so that the ground force could go in than trying to be a hero and shoot up the enemy on his own.

Without a shot fired at her, the Defender flew off.

When the four-man patrol gathered itself together, Spider said: "At long bleeding last!"

"Yeah," said Lawless. "Now they know where to come to find us."

"And the quicker the sooner," opined Trampas, cheerfully. "I could've knocked him out of the sky like a rotten tomato – "

"Sure, Trampas," Thwackers said. "Sure. And you'd have had your fool head blown off, believe you me."

"Nah. Never."

"Take a bet on it?"

Spider shook his head. "One of you'd never collect, that's for sure."

The normal taciturnity of Strike Force, relaxed of late, for this brief moment vanished. The relief from tension was indescribably wonderful. They felt like new men.

No longer were they perambulating targets. Now they could return to being what they were meant to be; professional soldiers, masters of their craft. The next time a chopper whirred over them the pilot, no matter how good he might be, wouldn't see them. The gunner would have no targets. And the chopper herself would be riddled with small arms fire. Yessir!

Thwackers flipped up his Scimitar pocket radio.

"Tom?"

"All okay?"

"Yeah. You saw the little beast?"

"Yes."

"He spotted us. Flew off to the east. No doubt his little brothers may come sniffing around."

"Right, Low Party. Rejoin."

None of the men in the four-man patrol of the Low Party was the least surprised that Tom Burnaby had not mouthed some rote formula of congratulation, even a simple 'Well done'. Of course they'd done well; but they'd merely done what they'd been sent out to do.

Now the whole of Strike Force had the rest of it to do.

CHAPTER TEN

From his vantage point Burnaby scanned the terrain below through the scope. A nice position had been selected on the forward slope among the grasses and tumbled rocks. Higher up a twisted mass of stone, some fifty or so metres off, was clearly the obvious place for an ambush to be set up.

So, equally obviously, Burnaby's section of Strike Force had eschewed it, burrowing in instead in this more forward position. Up among the lip of the crag the Whizz Kid had placed a few handy little bangers and smoke pellets. Come the time, they should look real good.

Smyjo came on the air

"Tom?"

"Yeah, Smyjo."

"They're doing it very nicely. We're following as per. You should see them in fifteen, twenty minutes."

"Right."

Burnaby wanted to check with Smyjo the possible presence of a hostile flanking force. If the Argies were doing it by the book they wouldn't all be clumped up into one bunch.

But – how to phrase the question in such a way that would not cause Smyjo's immaculate eyebrows to rise?

Eventually, Burnaby said: "No signs of any of 'em off to the flanks?"

"Only the standard flanking force. Nothing to worry about." Then Smyjo added: "They'll be on the far side of the main force. Thwackers and co should be able to deal with them."

"Right."

Odd how Burnaby just couldn't seem to get it right with Smyjo. The guardsman had it right himself. He wouldn't slip up. Burnaby cussed himself for a fool and settled back to wait.

Smyjo had with him Smart, Splodge and Taff.

The four-man patrol lying in wait here was composed of Hammer, Banjo, Q and the Whizz Kid. Sawbones, Burnaby had decided, should be kept with him and Andy, as a back-up group. As the OC, Burnaby wanted to be free to swing about. Three four-man patrols ought to be able to wreck the enemy group, even if they didn't account for them all.

Viewed from the air, the landscape with its shallow valleys, rocky outcrops and low hills might appear an expanse of deep green overtaken by golden brown. The few whirls of snow had no effect as yet on the colour scheme. The terrain might appear empty. Then the camouflaged-clothed men would be seen moving cautiously and swiftly from one place of concealment to the next, vanishing from sight at the end of each move.

Two parties were thus engaged.

One clung to the flank of the Argentine body, the other shepherded them on from the rear.

As for the Argentines themselves, as Smyjo radioed in, they did it correctly and by the book. They were professionals.

"No doubt they got their experience chasing dissidents and then shooting them when they'd surrendered."

"You think this bunch had a hand in all the disappearances?"

"Well, someone did, and a whole lot of Argentine

people just disappeared and were never heard of again. That's what a rotten government can do – like Hitler. Like those in some of the places in South East Asia."

Burnaby said: "Well, as far as we're concerned, they're just enemy troops. We treat 'em just as we would any other enemy."

Smyjo's reply was delayed. Then he said: "Right."

Burnaby fretted like a callow youth. Need he have said that?

Squatting up here in ambush gave a fellow far too much time to brood on unimportant matters. He must be getting paranoid about Smyjo. Every time he tried, every time he felt some rapprochement was in the offing, he screwed it up.

The biggest irony of all, of course, was his own conviction that Smyjo just was not aware at all of how Burnaby felt. To the big guardsman, Burnaby was another member of Strike Force, a trusted comrade.

Ironic – or just plain foolish?

The aerial view would now show the Argentines about to push into the valley where their helicopter reconnaissance had reported the presence of a British patrol.

Low Party out on the opposite side from Burnaby would have the extra complication of the Argie's left flank force. Was there then no right flank force?

Smyjo had sounded confident in his usual breezy way, and in this situation Burnaby trusted him. There was no question of likes and dislikes here. The man knew his job. Burnaby was convinced the Argies had not put out a right flank force, but were using the two-prong echelon. He found himself hoping that Low Force would not have to chew on too large a bite.

The biggest problem was the light.

Daylight – or the milky, murky, shifting approximation to daylight – would not last for much longer.

The job would have to be done sharpish.

Burnaby found himself urging on the Argentines as though they were a bunch of horses neck-and-neck for the winning post at Epsom.

Thwackers came on the air.

"Flank force is getting damned close, Tom."

Instantly Burnaby summed up Thwackers' predicament.

If the Argie flank force contacted Low Party early the balloon would go up before the main force was engaged. That, after all, was the function of the flank force.

"Can you haul off for five minutes, Thwackers?"

"Five is all."

"Right."

Smyjo came on. "Five will do it, Tom."

"Check."

In those five minutes Burnaby found himself thinking of Miss Anne Havisham. He did not want to think of her just then. He was all set to blast away at other human beings, to blow them apart. The two sets of thoughts ran incongruously in his head.

Remembering the heat of that summer afternoon he felt the warmth seeping along his bones. The vicar was away at a Diocesan conference of some sort. Anne led him into the hall, its coolness seemed refreshing, then but now, in rememberance, interfered with the joys of remembered warmth.

"I can offer you some sherbet."

"I haven't had sherbet since – oh, since I was a kid. Thank you."

They went into the kitchen, furnished in units of pale pine, lots of copper pans, a string of onions, flowers in pale blue vases, herb and spice racks, African violets on the windowsill.

"Mrs. Humbleton does for father; but I like to cook." The sherbet was provided in tall plain glasses. The fizz tickled deliciously.

The scents of the garden wafted in through the open window. The floor shone.

"You were going to explain your reprehensible conduct."

At once Burnaby relaxed. He recognized the gambit, the words conveying her tentative feeling that, well, perhaps this enormous husky man wasn't the raping kind.

He explained how his zip betrayed him, how he stumbled against Claire, how she had completely misunderstood the situation.

"She really clouted me."

"We used to fight each other, when we were girls. It's been useful."

"H'm. What is more important is – what's wrong? Claire is in trouble, I'm sure of it. Do you know?"

She said: "You know Claire has a marvellous job in the City – she's a P.A. to a most important person."

"Your father told me."

She ran a finger around the lip of her glass.

As he watched her, Burnaby realized she knew that Claire was a stripper but also that she was not going to admit it to a stranger. He decided to let her carry on for a little time yet. He was learning all the time.

She spoke rather more rapidly than she wanted to. "Claire – she's always been headstrong. She's the pretty one." She shot him a look under her eyelashes, and then took off the straw hat. "She – she had gambling debts."

This was quite unexpected.

Anne's hair, which previously Burnaby had seen screwed back into a severe bun, was now released from that efficient if blighting knot. It clustered about her face and gave her an altogether different look. The hair was still mousy, her face still pallid; but she was not wearing her glasses and she looked – different.

"When you accosted me at the swimming pool, Mr. Burnaby, I took you for one of the men who were trying to – to find Claire and make her pay."

"I see."

He didn't see it all. She and Claire had driven off to that country house where Claire had been forced into taking part in a stag video. Just how badly raw the picture might be Burnaby didn't know. He was not particularly interested. But he could see now that if Claire owed debts then that was the pressure which forced her to make the porno film.

The legality of the situation might be open to question; but there was no doubt the men who owned the gambling club would collect – one way or another.

"The only thing to do then, Miss Anne, is to pay up." He put the empty glass down on the scrubbed pinewood table. "Is – ah – is the – ?"

"Mr. Burnaby. I do not know why – it is most odd – " She passed the back of her hand across her forehead. All that pallid strained look returned to her face, the aura of serene contentment vanished. "I do not understand myself. Why I am even talking to you about private matters. But – but – three thousand pounds."

"Nasty."

"I have paid what I can – but my salary is not overly generous. And Claire – "

He interrupted. He'd made up his mind.

"Miss Anne. I am going to be frank – you could say brutally frank. I want to help Claire. I don't have that kind of money lying about loose, either. But I can help, somehow. May I say that when Claire was insulted in the pub and I was able to help her, I was not thinking of myself. Did she tell you why she was insulted?"

Anne drew in a breath. This, Burnaby saw, was what had been troubling her along with everything else.

"Surely, Mr. Burnaby, you did not believe what those

disgusting men said?"

Claire had been recognized by an unpleasant piece of work who had seen her doing her strip act and he had insisted she perform on the bar. Burnaby had put a stop to that exhibition of tasteless insult.

He said: "I interfered not because of that, but because Claire was in distress – "

Her head went up defiantly.

Gently, he said: "There are still situations in which women can be helped by men without losing their independence."

"But you didn't – "

"I have seen Claire at work."

She sagged. "Ah!"

He pushed on now with some vigour.

"So you can understand that your suspicions of me, although they may have been well-founded in your view, were quite groundless. I want only to be a friend to Claire, and you. And three thousand quid is right out of my league; but I'll scrape together what I can – "

"Mr. Burnaby! That is out of the question!"

Well, it was, really. But he couldn't see much else to be done.

"The thing is," he said, and in his ears his own voice sounded thin. "We don't want a dirty picture of Claire being circulated. Do we?"

"It's not dirty!"

He stared at her.

She bit her lip.

Then: "There is nothing wrong in nudity, Mr. Burnaby. Or in love. Love is the highest expression of humanity. You clearly have the sort of mind that can see only dirt – "

"Claire was not happy, was she? She did not want to make this rotten picture, did she?"

"Oh – how d'you know?"

"I saw enough – "

"You *saw*?"

"I followed you and Claire to that house. I saw what was going on. If I'd had the gump, I'd have gone in and wrapped their stinking video cameras around their grimy little necks!"

"Mr. Burnaby! I think you had better leave!"

"I don't understand you. I thought you were trying to help your sister. Yet – "

"I really cannot talk any more."

She glanced over at the clock on the wall and that dent appeared between her eyebrows.

"Goodbye, Mr. Burnaby."

He breathed out hard through his nose. Then he saw the absurdity of the situation.

"All right. I'll be off. But – "

A voice called from the open kitchen door.

"Anne! You there, Anne?"

Burnaby swung about. Anne gasped.

Striding into the kitchen came Claire Havisham, radiant, filled with light, gorgeous.

And Burnaby heard Andy say: "About time. There they are, Tom."

CHAPTER ELEVEN

Shooting a person in the back to a man of Burnaby's temperament had once seemed anathema, a coward's trick. Nowadays, of course, if he had to shoot someone in the back he'd just be thankful they weren't shooting at him.

Anybody who joins the Forces other than merely to escape the poverty trap must have some idea, however nebulous, of his reasons, ambitions, desires. Being a good soldier is not the easy thing some folk would make out. Soldiers are not dummies. The ultra-modern fighting man surrounded by computers and lasers, radar and satellite-communications, still has as a functional part of his environmental equipment the trusty old bondouk and bagnet. The rifle and bayonet might be all but forgotten to the radar-operator, the Chieftain commander, the Rapier crew. To the men in the field, hand-to-hand weapons figure a little more prominently. To the men of Strike Force they were very often the front-line kit, the sole weapon, the only way.

Strike Force were about to bring down a deluge of small arms fire on the heads of the enemy.

If by shooting a foe in the back, Burnaby could save the life of one of his own men, then he had no option but to carry out the deed. It was ugly. It was a fact of war that could be deplored. But there wouldn't have been this particular war if the thoughtless Argentines hadn't started the damned mess.

With soldiers of the calibre of Strike Force there was no need of last-minute orders. No need to say: "Hold your fire," or: "Fire when I do," or, even: "Safety catches off."

SSF let the fifty- or sixty-strong group of enemy special forces move on down the valley until they were in the right position. Smyjo came on the air. "Ready when you are, Tom."

That was mere common sense. Thwackers complied.

Burnaby got the group in his sights. They were badly strung out. He waited a few moments, licked his lips which he would not have done had the climate been a few degrees colder – and wondered why, if they were doing this by the book, they were so evilly organized. They weren't sufficiently dispersed, they were clumped. That must come from chasing up dissidents, students and workers.

The snow's tentative attempts had disappeared. The clouds began to clear away. The low sun began to shine level rays across the valley. The weather was taking an unexpected turn for the better, although it was still damned cold.

Burnaby pressed the trigger.

Instantly the rest of his group opened up.

Over on the opposite flank, Low Party joined in. Thwackers did say to himself a silent: "About bloody time."

The least satisfactory aspect of the operation lay in Smyjo's position to the rear and to the east of the Argentines. Like a shepherd his patrol would round up the enemy with the full eagerness of sheep dogs; but the declining rays of the sun burned directly into their eyes.

Out there in the valley dark figures were running and

stumbling, falling. Arms lifted in supplication. The acrid bite of smoke cut into men's throats, and the harsh rattle of gunfire seemed to vibrate in the very blood vessels of their brains.

The Argies were shooting back.

The Whizz Kid took quiet pride in his skills. He set off his bangers and smoke pellets along the crest among the ragged skyline. No great genius was required to see that the enemy, pinned in the valley, would see that rocky crest as the ambush position. There were men enough with courage out there to shoot back.

The enemy special forces group took cover, went to ground, got into firing position – and opened up.

Burnaby was annoyed. Despite all his own experiences and Smyjo's warnings, he had hoped the Argies would just run away.

Now the situation could go ugly.

There were fifteen blokes in Strike Force, fourteen of them armed. There must be fifty or so Argies out there, depending how many had been incapacitated after the first shots. Burnaby had to take into account the fact that Smyjo was not yet properly in action. He'd have a tough job if the Argies pulled back.

The situation was still fluid. A mortar would have come in handy now. Perhaps a rifle grenade, although they had for some reason gone out of fashion, could have chivvied 'em up. Targets were difficult to spot now. The Argies, wearing their funny little woollen caps, were well camouflaged and able to go to ground.

Smyjo came on the air.

"We've tickled 'em up, Tom. There's not much more percentage in this for us."

This was Burnaby's thought, yet because it was Smyjo who had voiced it, he had to say: "A few more casualties might persuade them, Smyjo."

The moment the words left his lips and were carried by

radio to Smyjo, he knew he'd committed a blunder. The Whizz Kid's pyrotechnics had banged and smoked to quiescence by now; all the same, Low Party and Smyjo's patrol had not had that luxury of not being shot at for a time. Knowing his own thoughts were confused, Burnaby had to make the right decision.

Before Smyjo could answer, Burnaby made up his mind. He spoke as though he merely continued what he had been saying, so fast had been all this mental turmoil.

"Pull your patrol back when you judge it right, Smyjo. Thwackers? Same applies. Let me know."

"Right."

Bullets continued to click and crack between the opposing groups. The sun slipped down further. Had this been a night-time operation the whole picture would have been different, vastly different. Burnaby had ideas for the night. With only four men on the flank and rear of the hostiles, he did not have a massive fire-front to bear. Pulling back was bad medicine; Burnaby judged he had to regard this decision as prudent.

The careful stalk, the decoy afforded by Low Party, the shepherding and then the ambush – all these careful preparations need not necessarily be wasted.

A slug caromed off a rock by his head.

Chips of stone flew, and a tiny fragment stung him on the cheek.

Out there in the valley the enemy had positioned themselves into a defence box. They were letting off their weapons at a prodigious rate.

In a low voice, Andy commented: "If they go on like that they'll run out of ammo. Then we just walk in and take their surrender."

"Sounds nice."

"You hit, Tom?" Burnaby realized he had put up his hand, and brought it away with the tip of his middle finger gleaming darkly red in the last of the light.

"Tiddler."

Andy triggered three careful shots, then ducked down. "Let's have a look-see."

"It's nothing – "

"Sure, sure."

Andy nicked out the chip of stone and clicked his tongue. Burnaby tried to pull away. He spat on his finger and rubbed his cheek.

"I'll call you a broody hen in a minute, Andy."

More shots ricocheted around. Splinters of stone flew through the air. Smyjo came on again.

"We're pulling back, rally point Able."

"Check."

Thwackers said: "Rally point Able, Tom."

"Check."

Burnaby twisted around. He felt thoroughly dissatisfied.

This unexpected clearance in the weather must take a deal of the blame. The brilliant sunshine, illuminating every feature of the slopes, made movement chancy. Even with night sights trained on the surrounding terrain, the Argies would not have spotted Strike Force with quite the same ease as they would now, should an advance be made.

It was frustrating.

It was also bloody annoying.

The soughing sound of the wind dropped for a moment and in that relative space of quietness a distant droning attracted everyone's absorbed attention. But then the wind returned, and the sound was drowned.

"Not a chopper," said Andy.

"No."

Sawbones wriggled down, hauling his kit.

"I vote we find a hole and pull the earth in on top."

"Got to find a better 'ole, Sawbones, before we do that … "

They crabbed along the slope, taking turns to bang off a few shots until they had gone too far to continue the impression that they had not moved at all. The Argentine special forces would know by now that the British were running away.

The western horizon resembled a blood bath. The setting sun shone streamers of fire through freshly driven cloud banks, and the westerly wind piled up the vapour into contused masses. Just after sunset the weather would resume its normal aspect. Again the breeze died and in the interval the droning sound from the east built in intensity. Then the wind scythed back and the sound was lost.

"Bleeding Pucara," said Andy.

"That's what I make it."

"Whistled up by those johnnies over there."

Burnaby considered. "He'll be on a sortie that'll get him back to base before true dark. We don't have a lot of time."

In that barren landscape going to ground was a matter of careful thought and preparation. Everything had to look right from the air.

Burnaby called up the other two patrols and checked that they were fully alive to the perils of the coming situation.

"No sweat," said Thwackers. "We're like bugs in a rug."

"Anti-surveillance routine in force, Tom," confirmed Smyjo.

It felt colder now. Their ponchos proved just that little bit more difficult to handle. Air cut into the lungs. The metal parts of their weapons were wrapped as far as possible in scrim, taped up, as much against the cold as for camouflage.

They went to ground as the sound of the aircraft purred in, swelling, dominatng the rushing of the wind.

They would have to sweat out this attack before they could assemble at rally point Able.

Hunkered down and with an eyeball aimed up through the gap between poncho and peaty soil, feeling the wetness of the scrape around him, Burnaby watched evilly for the first sign of the Pucara. The plane flew into sight, skimming low over the ground. Her propellers glinted into silver discs. She looked predatory. If a Harrier happened to show up, the Pucara would turn into a frightened quarry hypnotised by a bird of prey. But there were no friendly Harriers around now.

His breath caught in his throat.

The plane flew on.

If the Argies seized their chance and doubled up, they could catch the Brits with their pants down. The Major used to say, among other things, that the men of Strike Force were never caught with their pants down, even in the lavatory.

"I'm fed up with this," Burnaby said. "Andy, we'll have to go at the blighter if he comes back."

"Too right."

Q and the rest of his patrol expressed themselves delighted at the opportunity. Everyone felt the frustration of the past hour. Hitting back at this insolent bird who carried such a punch would relieve the blood pressure.

They could hear the Pucara, her engines droning as she flew in a wide circle. By that sound they could roughly estimate her position. She was turning to fly back.

Burnaby could feel his heart thumping, big heavy pulsations that travelled through his body. He peered up. His face showed no expression – anybody looking at him would recognize only craggy determination.

"Wait until she's right on top of us."

No one answered. They all knew the drill. Wait until

the plane was almost overhead and then open up. That way she'd have no chance to shoot at them and would be too far ahead in her course to drop bombs.

The waiting had to be endured.

The noise of the twin engines swelled.

Burnaby stuck up his head a little higher and used both eyes.

He felt like cursing.

The Pucara flew back at a higher altitude than when she'd skimmed low over them the first time.

Strike Force was up from the ground, weapons snouting. They took aim and shot, carefully, tracking the aircraft, expending full magazines in the effort, trying to bring her down by sheer volume of fire.

But she flew on, turning sharply. She tilted on a wing, a black cross reddened by the sun's setting glow. Her propellers spun orange-silver. She banked superbly, levelled out, tracked dead centre on their group.

"Not a sausage," said Andy, ramming in a fresh magazine. He lifted his rifle again – and froze.

"Oh, my Christ!" he said.

Burnaby saw. There was time to feel sick right down to his stomach. He felt green.

From the Pucara spilled two cigar-shaped objects.

They tumbled over in the air, seeming to take for ever as they floated down. The plane was a flashing blur of distorted colour. The two tanks were spinning down towards the men below.

"Napalm!"

CHAPTER TWELVE

Tucked in behind Lawless, Spider tramped on for rally point Able.

The banks of cloud ahead partially obscured the reddened disc of the sun; the whole world was far too brightly lit for Spider's comfort.

Bringing up the rear of Low Party, Thwackers constantly rotated his head, checking the back trail. Like this, his patrol was silhouetted like a bunch of idiot targets.

They kept low.

Trampas hacked along, trying not to think of anything much. It was going to be a bastard of a night.

Spider couldn't help his thoughts mockingly dwelling on what Andy would inevitably say about the evening's entertainment. The sergeant major in his most majestic manner would with absolute certainty pronounce:

"A monumental cock-up."

It was.

They heard the aeroplane in the shifting lulls of the cutting wind. The sound seemed to emanate from where Tom and the main party were heading in for rally point Able.

No one needed to be told what to do if the aircraft nosed inquisitively over Low Party. Thwackers was more concerned about those Argie special forces blokes showing more of the courage they had displayed in the valley. The droning of engines grew louder.

"There he is," said Lawless.

Spider squinted across.

A small black shape flitted above the ground, turning with a glinting of reddened silver light, swinging around and climbing. Low Party could see the plane clearly in that streaming orange radiance.

"Pucara."

"Yeah. Nasty little beasts."

"He's got to be near Tom."

"Somewhere near."

With a careful look back to make sure the trail remained clear, Thwackers joined the others in staring at that evil little aeroplane as it banked around again.

They saw the rolling orange flames, the boiling black smoke. Gobbets of vivid flame coruscated along the ground. Swirls of flame and smoke covered and broke in a pulsating pandemonium of horror. The booming explosions reached them almost immediately. They stood there, watching; they couldn't speak.

One word stood starkly in all their minds.

"Napalm!"

*

"Napalm!"

Calculations flowed effortlessly through his head: ballistic trajectories, time to drop, angles of impact. The terror goaded him into frenzied activity. Burnaby screamed as he threw himself forward.

"This way! *Jump*!"

The Pucara was high; the pilot had delayed a fraction in dropping his tanks of horror. The cigar-shaped cylinders tumbled through the air in an obscene travesty of an underwater ballet. They would hit off to the left and forward of the group of men.

Burnaby ran like a crazy man back along the track the aircraft had taken, directly under and away. The others followed without thought. Yelling with bursting lungs, Burnaby simply thrashed himself away from hell, driven by a panic so vast as to fill his entire being.

He leaped over the ground until through the fear-crazed thoughts the realization caught up with him that he daren't risk another yard in this upright position. He hurled himself forward and down, hugging the earth, trying to burrow into the soil with his bare hands.

Already he curled away inside from what was to come. Already he could feel the crisping heat, the searing flash, his skin burning and melting, his lungs on fire and collapsing ...

Flat against the earth he hugged himself, cringing.

The explosions were merely big bangs. They meant little. The heat – the suffocation – the stinking feeling of the air being dragged away from him, burning, burning ...

He could feel the flames roaring and twisting above. He could see the ground beneath him lit as though by an inferno coruscating just above his head. His eyes squeezed shut. Tears poured out. His body shook.

The roar of flames persisted. The heat swelled and then – unbelievably, wonderfully, miraculously – began to ease. His back stung. His boots felt tight. His hands, clenched into futile fists, grasped at the soil. He shook with terror. He survived.

Survival meant opening his eyes.

The whole of his chest felt as though he had inhaled pure flame. He had not. He had grasped correctly the point of impact and had taken evasive action. The tanks had fallen, exploded and bounced forward with their momentum far enough away from him to distance the full effects. The men with him were shaken, shattered, bathed in heat. But the flames had not touched them. The air swooshed and whistled past, drawn in to feed the fires. Coldness and heat mingled oddly.

Rolling over, he looked up. His vision, blurred by tears, revealed a darkly blue, red-tinged expanse covering him.

Blinking, wiping his eyes, he got himself back in order. He felt as though he'd been beaten all over. His knees still shook.

Back there, the napalm burned with gyrating shifts and roilings of flame and smoke. The heat clawed at him. Andy crawled across, his grimy face stained by the tracks of tears. Burnaby looked just the same.

The noise dwindled. The conflagration blew away. Evil died.

Andy did not sit up; he twisted to stare at Burnaby.

"Soldiers just do not *like* napalm," he said.

His voice was a croak.

"Anybody hurt?"

Speaking was an effort. His throat gripped with a dry pain. He could not bring up a single spot of spittle. The feeling of fire in his head and lungs would take a long time to go away.

Between them, the men sorted themselves out.

All of them possessed quick reflexes. They would not have been selected for Strike Force if they had been sluggards. Burnaby's yell and his instant movement had spurred them all to follow. They'd all escaped the full effects; had they been very much nearer to the point of impact and on the other side they'd all be dead. Only Hammer had caught a nasty result; he lay gasping for breath, his face bloated, eyes staring, unable to speak.

What had happened to him was clear enough from his position. In his frantic dive for cover he'd hit the side of a clumpy outcrop and twisted over so that the heat slapped at his face, upturned as he fell. With delicate care, they doctored him with ointments, bandaged him up, tried to make him comfortable.

Inside himself Burnaby could feel the frozen horror of it all and rage at his own futility. Sure, he'd read the situation aright and yelled and set an example. But he could not forget the terror that had overwhelmed him. that would take time to fade, to stop troubling him. He felt, in those ghastly moments, that the sensations would never leave him.

Into Hammer's ear, Burnaby said: "Press my hand if you can see."

Relief shocked through Burnaby as he felt Hammer's fingers grip into his.

Thank God for that!

"We'll have to whistle up a casevac," he said. Speaking was still difficult. "If the radio is still useable."

Checking over what they had available would have to wait for a time. The Pucara had flown off after that devastating attack and, although the sun was now almost gone, there was no guarantee that the plane would not return for a final check of the damage caused and a last machine gun attack.

Trying to look out and understand what he saw was damned difficult. He couldn't stop blinking. His eyes felt like hot pebbles. He couldn't see the Pucara although faintly he could hear her engines.

He thought he heard a few pop-popping noises as well; but they were short-lived and quickly died away.

The savage desire possessed him to have had a Blowpipe in his fists, to lift the rocket launcher to his shoulder and bring the Pucara down in flames as he had shot down that poor devil in his Skyhawk. That would have been the result Strike Force looked for.

The rest of the main party gathered like a bunch of shipwrecked sailors staggering ashore on a desert island. They were partially deafened, half-blinded, shattered. But they were alive. Being alive, being soldiers of Strike Force, they soldiered on.

Burnaby, for one, pushed aside the uneasy imaginings of what this and similar hair-raising occurrences might do to his nerves and intestinal tracts in the future. He might get himself killed tomorrow and never have a future in which to be a nerve-stricken war veteran.

Thwackers came on the air, sounding awful.

"Yeah," said Burnaby, straining to hear the radio voice. "We're all okay. Hammer took a burn, though."

"Spider took a shot at the bastard when he flew away. There was a smidgin of smoke from his port engine. Maybe one of you heroes winged him."

"Maybe."

After that Smyjo radioed in.

"Okay, Smyjo. We're calling for a casevac for Hammer."

"I am greatly relieved. When we saw – well, never mind that. I'm not coming in tonight. We're stalking the Argies. We've got them under obbo and I want to know where they're hiding out."

"Good, Smyjo."

As he spoke Burnaby felt his own dog-tiredness, and wondered – not for the first time – where Smyjo got all his bounding energy from. Bran and whole grain for breakfast?

Banjo got the big Scimitar radio working and they called up HQ.

"I know you have logistic problems," Burnaby told Noggy at the other end. Noggy still had his busted ribs strapped up. If he insisted on falling off a submarine into the freezing waters of the South Atlantic, he must expect to be out of the campaign. For all that, being of the usual stubborn pattern of a Strike Force man, Noggy soldiered on at HQ.

"Problems and a half, Tom."

"Well, it's Hammer up here. He needs hospitalization, Noggy. Rustle up a casevac as soon as you can, hey?"

"Will do."

There was no further cheery conversation, and enquiries after the others, no false heroics. Each knew what was going on, each knew what had to be done.

Later on, during the night, Noggy came on again to report that he had organized a casualty evacuation helicopter for first light. That eased Burnaby's problems. He had no wish to lose Hammer, and if he thought of Pugsy being so hideously killed, well, he wouldn't even begin to understand his own emotions. Hammer would go out with the casevac and he'd recover. Pugsy was buried somewhere over there on the mainland.

With Low Party rejoined, Strike Force awaited news from Smyjo's patrol.

This stubborn recovery from near disaster represented a living force Burnaby understood, a trait of character he could admire. He hadn't realized Claire Havisham possessed that strength of resolution even with the evidence before him. Needing to earn a living, and without real skills, she had taken up stripping. She was good at her job. She was also a consummate actress, following the sweetness and light path when at home in the vicarage, acting the stripper when on stage. When was she herself?

She'd come waltzing into the kitchen, bathed in sunshine, radiant, smiling. He'd stared at her, and if he was spellbound, well, wasn't that a normal masculine reaction to such feminine beauty?

"Tom Burnaby!"

The smile slipped.

"Hello, Claire. Anne and I were just talking about you."

"Then you will do me the favour of leaving my house at once. I want nothing more to do with you – "

Anne spoke up.

"Claire! It's – it's not quite as easy as that. I was just

asking Mr. Burnaby to leave. But not for the reasons you might expect – "

Burnaby couldn't stand any more of this noxious formality. Both girls were looking at him with expressions they might have used to inspect what they'd picked up on the soles of their shoes.

He took a breath. He even put his hands on his hips, clenched into fists. He felt the blood in his face.

"Now, listen to me! You, Claire, and you, Anne – to hell with the formalities! Claire – you're in trouble through gambling, and you're a stripper, and you're making a porno video. I'd guess you don't want to make it. If I'm right, why the blue-blazing hell won't you let me help you?"

Anne put a hand to her mouth. Claire stood bolt-upright, bright-faced, unmoving, staring at him.

"Well?"

"You may shout all you like, Mr. Burnaby – "

He was tempted to use words more suited to toms tabbing up an ice slope in Norway and falling arse-over-tip into icy sludge. He breathed in. He breathed out. Then:

"I did not try to rape you. I did not even make an advance to you. It was my confounded zip – no. Let me finish. If you really do so detest me that you and Anne cannot bear the sight of me, then I'll be off. All I want to do is what is right. If we can scrape the cash together we can stop this rotten film, can't we? Isn't that what you really want?"

Her eyes were so bright now they filled his vision.

"Tom – it's – I thought ... The film is awful! I didn't know what ... "

"Claire!" Anne moved towards her sister, and stopped.

"The things they made me do – they said they'd tell Father – they said they'd mark me – they said – "

She swayed. Then, quietly, she started to sob.

Burnaby said: "Right. That's settled, then."

He could understand stubborn pride, and how it could reach a point where the strain at last proved too great. When Smyjo came on the radio the relief was akin to that of tears.

"They're located in an abandoned set of farm buildings in the middle of nowhere."

"Good – "

"They're having a high old time. It's absolutely freezing out here, and they've got fires going, showing lights like there's no tomorrow. We can even smell cooking mutton – three sixty five the kelpers call it, don't they? The Argies really are settled in like the new owners."

"Not," said Burnaby, "for long."

"I quite agree, old boy."

"I'm not hanging about. I'll bring a patrol along right away. As soon as Hammer is evacuated the rest can hack across."

Smyjo sounded pleased. He passed over directions, routes were arranged, and then Burnaby said: "Password is 'Hammer'. Out."

Throughout the campaign helicopters proved expensive and much-sought after items. Some worked splendidly, others, of which much had been expected, surprisingly turned out not to be so wonderful after all. The Aerospatiale Gazelle was fitted with a pintle-mounted jimpy by the marines, the left-hand door being removed and the gun and mount taken from the Volvo BV.202 snow vehicle. SNEB/Matra 68mm rocket pods were also fitted to some Gazelles. Unfortunately, the helo lacked a stabilized magnifying sight so she couldn't hover off out of range of hostile small arms fire.

When, just after first light, the casevac flew in, the pilot – an extremely competent individual – made no overt comments. The lack of cabin space was plain, and the chopper looked as fragile as she proved.

Q had done his nut to obtain a few extra supplies to make up for those lost during then napalm attack, and to secure fresh ammunition for the force's weapons. Hammer was safely seen off after Sawbones had given him a final check-over, much like the proverbial mother hen.

By that time Burnaby, Banjo, Andy and the Whizz Kid had reached the hide set up by Smyjo which overlooked the farm settlement. As Smyjo had said, it was cold. The snow that had been threatening on and off must soon start. The Argies were either careless about lights, or indifferent. Perhaps they were perfectly confident.

"They can set up fields of fire down there and chop any open attack," commented Smyjo.

He and Burnaby lay with their heads either side of a clump of grasses, using their night sights, trying to see if anything interesting was going on. The day, or what there was of day, was due soon.

"Then we'll have to be sneaky." Burnaby felt the need to square off with Smyjo. He wanted to get the record straight. So, without the hesitation he expected to hear in his own voice, he said: "This time we'll mallet 'em properly. Made a bit of a pig's dinner of the ambush. I am not at all happy about that."

Smyjo did not turn. "Happens, old son. You weren't to know that the sun would come out like that."

"All the same – "

"Don't fret, old boy. No gelt in that."

That was the trouble with Burnaby and Smyjo; Burnaby just couldn't seem to adapt to what Smyjo's attitude would be. He remained unpredictable. This conversation was not going the way Burnaby had anticipated.

Collecting his thoughts, Burnaby studied the terrain

surrounding the isolated farm.

The dawn light, freakish, miserable, crept up over the rim of the world. By now they could see without the aid of night vision equipment. The lights in the farm building and the adjoining sheds glowed wanly for a time and then were extinguished. Smoke rose.

"Mutton, did you say, Smyjo?"

"Yes. Had a sniffing session down there."

For anybody else in Strike Force, Burnaby's answer might have been some rude, crude near-joke about glue. For Smyjo he could not bring himself to the required frame of mind.

"Can't see any sentries."

"Couple of blokes at the window, I shouldn't wonder."

"Yes."

"Look, Tom, don't let the ambush worry you. Okay, so it was what Andy would call a monumental cock-up. But don't blame yourself!"

Burnaby lay still, watching the farm buildings. If he had not been in control of himself, he'd have been grinding his teeth so hard they'd have crumbled to powder.

CHAPTER THIRTEEN

Towards late morning a couple of sentries appeared at the door of the farmhouse. They were clad in the generous parkas of the Argentine soldiery, carried rifles, and they took up positions in the prescribed fashion to cover anyone approaching.

Shortly thereafter the sound of a helicopter announced visitors.

"Those two events," Splodge said to his oppo Taff, "are indisputably connected."

"Putting on a good show for the high brass."

"They're cocky, these Argie special forces blokes. Too damned cocky by half."

The two were on obbo, concealed in a rim of scattered boulders overlooking the farm. The helicopter appeared, swooped in, hovered, and settled on a flat patch of ground at some distance from the station buildings. Burnaby, who had caught forty winks, crawled up to have a look-see at the excitement, and was shortly joined by Smyjo.

From the helicopter a single man emerged.

From the station buildings another single man walked out, briskly rubbing his hands.

Everyone expected the new arrival to go across to his welcoming committee and then go inside the building.

Instead, he waited by the chopper for the man from the farm to join him. Then, unexpectedly, they began to walk slowly away from the helo, away from the buildings, towards the rocks. They had their heads together as though talking earnestly, and they walked casually, not hurrying.

Burnaby said: "Smyjo. We can crawl along behind this ridge. If those two come any closer – "

"They won't see us for sure."

Without further words they began to edge along in the cover of the stones and tufty grass. They reached the spot opposite the line of advance of the two Argies below, and hunkered down. Looking up, all that might be observed from below would be a couple of pairs of eyeballs.

Smyjo and Burnaby waited as the Agentines drew closer.

The quick flow of Spanish was completely lost on Burnaby. He said nothing. Smyjo was listening; anything that was said down there was going into Smyjo's receptive ears and being stored in his brain.

Presently, Smyjo said: "Tom – they're planning – "

"Schtumm!"

Smyjo stopped speaking as though he'd ridden into a brick wall. He seemed to gather himself like a jaguar on a branch ready to spring down on the unsuspecting head of his prey. He remained motionless.

Then, the man from the helo said: "My English is not – not so good, Peter. But you are – sure – confident – ?"

"Absolutely, old chap," said the man from the farm buildings. He spoke in a cut-glass voice, very brisk and altogether English. "We speak English a lot at home. We used to think it kept us in touch with the Mother Country."

The accent was not altogether English; the lilt of Welsh sounded, and the overtones of South American life gave just a tinge of foreignness.

To himself, Burnaby said: "An Anglo-Argentine.

H'm. Poor devil. His loyalties were tugged about a bit."

The Anglo-Argentine half-turned so that he was fully facing the hide where Burnaby lay. "There will be no difficulty in the language. And if you have a reasonable uniform for me I can foresee no great problems. Afterwards, of course … "

The helicopter man resumed in Spanish, and Burnaby started to chew over what the hell was going on.

His first impressions of the man called Peter were of a hard, regular-featured face, handsome, with a heavy black moustache curling downwards in the South American fashion. The man looked fit and strong, good-looking, no doubt a ladies' man. His body being enclosed in a bulky anorak made no difference to the impression of sturdiness.

After a few more moments of coversation in Spanish, the Argentines began to stroll back towards the helicopter.

Although they were out of earshot now, Smyjo did not speak. Burnaby's rebuke had been harsh enough, the Lord knew. From the helicopter another man emerged. The three of them stood talking and gesticulating, and then the man called Peter slapped the newcomer on the back and climbed up into the chopper.

The man to whom he had been speaking said a few last words – Burnaby could guess easily enough what they'd be – and then the newcomer started briskly off for the farmbuildings.

Whoever he was, the chappie who'd flown in in the chopper was important. He climbed into the helicopter, the door closed, and the blades began to revolve. In a chuntering roar and a breeze of broken grass stems and muck, the chopper lifted away. She set course due east.

Burnaby shifted back from the crest line and rolled over. He pushed himself up and turned a hard eye on Smyjo.

"Well?"

"Diabolical, diabolical."

"Yes. I gather the bloke called Peter who speaks English is to be fitted out with a British uniform. A spy."

"A damned sight more than that, old boy." Smyjo was in command of himself now. He passed a rigid forefinger over his upper lip. "He was asked if he would accept a special mission. He agreed. His orders are to dress up as a British officer, infiltrate our positions, and then to kill the GOC."

"Kill the general!"

"That's right. The dirty bastards – "

Burnaby could be far more philosophical about the side effects of warfare than the guardsman.

"Oh, I don't know. Remember, we had a go at Rommel. War's a dirty business. You can't blame the Argies."

"But think what it means! The GOC's going to go in danger of his life – "

"Don't we all?"

"Yes, yes. But not like this!"

"My guess is that the GOC will shrug this off. He's a tough bird. He'll have an escort, and this Peter what's-his-name will be picked off before he gets a shot."

"Ye-es – I suppose you're right."

Burnaby had never seen Smyjo like this. He seemed to have taken personally this pathetic Argie assassination attempt.

"We'll radio HQ. Noggy will pass on the gen. They'll set up security as tight as a virgin. But, I think, Smyjo, it does mean one thing."

"Yes?"

"One of us will have to go to GHQ and describe this fellow. Got to make absolutely sure."

They both knew at once who would have to go.

Smyjo thumped a gloved fist into his palm.

"That means I'll miss all the fun from now on."

" 'Fraid so."

Smyjo closed his lips. He did not look a happy man.

Burnaby said in his mild voice: "He'll have to shave that moustache though, or trim it. He could make himself look like a British officer, a para, say, without much trouble."

"The gang in the Maroon Machine just about know everyone, don't they? It's like a club."

"In the middle of a campaign this assassin chappie will have as good a chance as any of passing without being recognized for what he is. Come on, let's get to the wireless."

Smyjo scrambled back down the slope and then half-rose. He stared up as Burnaby followed.

"Another thing, Tom."

"Oh?"

"Puzzles me. I couldn't quite catch the drift of what they were saying. I think they were speaking as though if what they were planning came out they could deny ever having spoken."

"What?"

"Something about if it all went wrong, if things got really bad, then the alternative solution would have to be applied."

"That all?"

"Yes. From the way they talked, they're both very strong-minded men. They believe in what they're doing and they're prepared to be ruthless to get what they want. No one is going to stand in their way. Even if he is the British GOC."

Noggy sounded incredulous as they passed on the news, and then convinced. The Scimitar wobbled up and down the wavelengths in a fantastic pattern that defied interception. All the same, the men of Strike Force habitually used few words, and cryptic ones at that.

Q said: "You'll have to get a chopper in to take Smyjo out." He rubbed his hands, and bent to the mike.

"Noggy. This is Q. Pack aboard everything you can lay your hands on." He went on to describe in the glowing terms of a mail order catalogue the assortment of deadly items he wanted. What Strike Force had begun with had been mostly shot off by now.

It was arranged for Smyjo to hack back a few miles so as to clear any possible observation of the chopper by the Argies. The big guardsman was in a subdued mood.

He said to Burnaby: "Y'know, Tom, the Anglo-Argentinians are in a dicey position. They've remained proud of having this British ancestry; and they've based their success in Argentina on commercial good sense. What they don't like to be reminded of is the fact that their ancestors were not aristocracy, were in general the poor classes who cleared out of the mother country; servants and labourers and people like that."

Burnaby said nothing.

Smyjo went on: "They're not all Welsh, as a lot of people falsely believe. They came from all over. The Irish, being Catholics, were even more successful. But they're fanatical about their cricket clubs and their Harrods and their tea-parties and all the details they believe apertain to British social class."

"Argentina," said Burnaby, "is their country. You can't really blame 'em for sticking up for their own country, can you? Even now, when as far as international law and the United Nations says, they're in the wrong."

"All set, Tom," Andy called across.

Burnaby looked over. "Who's going, then?"

"Smartie, Splodge, Taff – and me."

"Right. Take a breather before you hack back."

"Yeah."

Burnaby wasn't having a lone man of his command marching off across hostile country. A full patrol would escort Smyjo to the chopper landing point, and then hack back, fingers on triggers.

About a couple of kilometres, perhaps even one and a half, would be all that were necessary. The patrol, lugging the kit the chopper brought in, would be back in no time.

"Then," said Smyjo with some bitterness, "you'll rest up for the remainder of the night, and go in at first light. I ought to be with you."

Burnaby felt enormous relief when Andy, with a ferocious grimace that in Strike Force often passed for a smile, said: "We all have our crosses to bear."

Smyjo was seen off with all due ceremony, the patrol returned with the kit Q had drummed up, and the force got their heads down, apart from the routine rotation of an obbo team.

The weather turned nasty during the night.

Snug in his sleeping bag, Burnaby had to consider the condition of his men. The force had been operating at a high pitch for some time. The lads were hairy and grimy and tattered at the edges.

Working out who would do what during the attack consumed valuable time during which he could think professionally, and exclude all unwelcome thoughts. But his calculations were soon complete. Restlessly, he considered crawling out of his sack and checking everything. He rejected that idea. The blokes would give him an odd look, wonder if the captain was cracking up. They knew the job; he had the utmost faith in them. There was no need to go prowling around like a mother superior at a convent after lights out.

The idea occurred to him that he very often ran over in his mind the fact that these men of Strike Force were exceptional at their work. Lying there, he pondered on this for a moment, thought involuting upon itself. Did this betray a weakness in himself? He doubted it – he hoped he – no, dammit! It did not. He was just the worrying kind, he supposed.

He fretted over this stupid antipathy he felt for Smyjo. Mind you, it was not all that stupid when he considered Smyjo's dismissive remarks about the Anglo-Argentines and their ancestry. They'd made a success of their new lives in a fresh country, and wasn't that a matter of pride, all the more so if they'd originated in the working classes and hadn't had it all presented to them on a silver plate? In Burnaby's book they'd every reason to feel proud, not ashamed, of their forebears.

Anyway, when a country could produce a writer of the stature of Jorge Luis Borges, then something was working out all right. He turned over, and the wind went howling along in a most dire fashion. He'd worried over Claire Havisham. Scraping the barrel, they'd raised the three thousand. Sheila, with a dark muttering about: "Them awful lot," had chipped in. Paul, Claire's artistic fashion designer friend, had also helped. He could understand why they and Anne helped; his own motives were much more obscure.

She'd said: "No, Tom, thank you. I'd better go along to the club and pay them myself."

That sounded reasonable, so he'd agreed.

He'd had to go back and get on with the job of soldiering then, and had no word from Claire or Anne on how the business turned out. When he could get away he'd hired a car and driven down to see Anne. She remained his only direct link with Claire. Surprising him, Anne said she was on the way up to see Claire, Burnaby could drive her. That suited him, and they set off through an afterglow of the late summer day, all sweet scents and long shadows and the feeling of the year drawing in to autumn.

The warmth of the sleeping bag enclosed him and then he was aware of Spider ready to haul him out. He sat up and said: "Okay, Spider."

"It's brass monkeys, Tom."

Spider spoke no less than the truth. When Burnaby crawled out from under the poncho and stood up, the wind and cold hit him in the face like a blow from a mailed fist. A mailed fist covered in ice. He took one single gasp, then he was in command of himself and taking the necessary measures for his brain to instruct his body to ignore the cold. He'd allocated himself last watch, so as to be in position to monitor what was going on down at the farm buildings right up to the last minute. He crawled up to the obbo position and looked down.

He could see nothing, and the night sight revealed no movement.

It started to snow.

The wind eased up enough for the big flakes to drop silently, blown now and then by a gust, eventually to settle. The land turned a ghostly off-white grey. The dark clouds massed above, putting a sombre lid on the world. There was not a star to be seen.

Keeping warm was a technique often practised in unforgiving climates. Norway, Canada, places where you had to know what you were doing to stay alive. He checked his watch. In theory, first light was half an hour or so off. The troops worked off Greenwich Mean Time; but local time was useful. If the snow and the overcast sky persisted, the attack ought to be able to go in unobserved.

Without the need of a lot of shouting and rousing out the men of Strike Force gathered. They'd grabbed a little to eat; some did, some didn't. The imminence of fighting took men in different ways. They were quiet. They formed up into the two wings as Burnaby had ordered.

Left Flank Wing consisting of Q, the Whizz Kid, Trampas

and Banjo would act as the Fire Support Team.

The chopper sent to take out Smyjo had brought in a considerable quantity of the goodies ordered by Q, although not all. Q handed out the 66mm M72A1 Light Anti Armour weapons as though dispensing Christmas presents. The little rocket launchers might be withdrawn from NATO because they would be totally useless against Soviet T72s and T80s; they were doing damn good service down here in the Falklands. It was Q's opinion that if one of these LAWs smacked into a tank track then it would do that AFV a piece of no good at all, no matter how grand and thick the armour above.

Trampas intended to use his L4A2 LMG, which everyone called a Bren, and Banjo took possession of a rifle. Burnaby had included Banjo in the Fire Support Team for two reasons: one, he had no direct oppo now that Hammer had been casevaced and, two, he needed a signals wallah by the big set. Well – near it, for Banjo would inevitably get stuck in.

The fact that there were thirteen of them did not faze Burnaby at all. There were really only twelve. Sawbones would perform his usual invaluable functions, and would not count in the fire fight.

They set off, undramatically, snow billowing about them. They marched with their heads slanted against the white filth; they watched and they looked. They were, Burnaby considered, like a bunch of homicidal hoodlums on the prowl. But they were not maniacal murderers. They were professional soldiers out on a tough assignment, prepared to act as soldiers and do what was necessary to bring success – and not get themselves killed.

Q had six 66mm Laws. Right Flank Wing, who were the other eight members of Strike Force formed into two patrols, had two 66mm. As Burnaby stepped down the slope towards the farm buildings, he became aware of a distinct slackening in the wind force. It was less cold. It stopped snowing. They were only about seven minutes behind schedule, and he'd cleared that with Q over the wireless handsets. As the party marched on, fanning out to take up their positions on the start lines they had so well memorised, the wind dropped altogether. The clouds were staining rose and pink. First light was on them, and first light was heralding a fine day.

There was absolutely no use Burnaby blinding and swearing over this turn of events.

Strike Force was committed, and Strike Force would go in.

As the distorted disc of the sun punched up over the horizon and the day began, Q let rip with the first of his 66mm. The rocket lanced into the wooden farm buildings.

The second LAW slammed in, and the buildings began to burn.

Burnaby waved, and the whole line surged forward.

CHAPTER FOURTEEN

The powdering of snow crunched underfoot. Breaths steamed from their mouths; at each jagged leap forward they poised, and leaped on, puffing like locomotives.

Andy had one of the 66mm. Right Flank force was coming in almost at right angles, to give the fire team a clear field. Andy let rip, and the explosion tore a hole in the side of the building. Flames were already coiling up from the roof, and off from the left Q put in another rocket.

Trampas's Bren lay down a steady metronomic beat of fire as he ran through the 'Johnny-get-your-gun' drill.

For the moment Burnaby could see no targets, and so he held his fire. His men did likewise.

They ran on, ready on the instant to fling themselves flat into the snow.

There had been, as far as he could see, not a sign of a sentry outside the house. On the previous day the Argies had only put out sentries when the big boss flew in. Maybe they felt it was too darned cold to stand sentry-go.

From a window near the corner of the house and well away from the splintered hole knocked in by Andy, dark figures started to spill out, leaping out of the window. No doubt it was a trifle warm inside.

Smart's patrol opened up.

Burnaby continued to run forward with Andy, Spider

and Lawless. They angled around to the back of the house, leaving the front and side to the other patrols. The fourth side of the house possessed no windows or doors.

The sound of machine gun fire and the rattle of rifle fire grew. The smell of cordite stung; but in these conditions smelling became atrophied with the cold.

Men were falling into the snow, dropping from the window and not rising. From the front of the house, where Trampas had the door under continuous burst-fire, men tried to escape the inferno at their backs. They rushed out and were shot down.

Some got through. Brave, foolhardy, tough and not yet ready to give in, the Argies raced outside and threw themselves down and returned the deadly fire cutting them to pieces.

Q smacked in another 66mm. Flames billowed from the windows. The house blazed up, and the sketchy outbuildings joined in the conflagration.

A crack by Burnaby's ear made him hit the deck. Argies ran around the far corner where he was headed, shooting from the hip. Their sub-machine gun fire spattered into the snow about the British.

Lying prone, Burnaby opened up. His Personal Weapon cracked off, hitting into the dark group of enemies.

Others joined in. The fire fight brisked up into the dawn air.

A few Argies positioned themselves in the lee of a small shed just off to the side of the house. Andy lined up his last 66mm LAW and let fly.

The rocket streaked a bright trail that ended slap into the shed. It exploded like a trick Easter egg.

Everyone shot into the heart of the explosion.

Most of the Argies were dressed, wearing their anoraks. Some even had webbing in place. They continued to shoot from what positions they could scrabble from the snow and half-frozen ground outside the burning house. Bullets snapped and cracked.

Left Flank Wing put down covering fire in a neat pattern. Right Flank Wing stood up and charged forward, shooting, and then flopped down to reload and drag in a breath and gather themselves for the next effort.

Burnaby stuffed in a fresh mag, and decided that it would soon be grenade time.

Unfortunately – for the Brits, that was, not the Argies – Q had been unable for all his wiles and guile to obtain any M79 grenade launchers. Anyway, the 66mm LAWs had taken out the building. The grenades at that point would have been overkill.

The Argies were now shooting back with real venom; yet their fire was haphazard, sporadic, and vilely aimed.

They'd been caught disastrously with their pants down, to use the Major's imagery. The fact that they were wearing anoraks, and yet were supposed to be special forces, indicated their regard for the severity of the weather. The sun was still only just about lifting above the horizon. The light lay clear and chill upon the frozen land. Burnaby, reloaded, ready to go, took a breath and leaped up, lunged forward.

He heard Trampas let off a string of rounds in that thum-thum-thump characteristic of the Bren. Evidently Trampas had given up the 'Johnny-get-your-gun' routine and was just hosing it in. With him Banjo, Q and the Whizz Kid slammed their slugs towards the enemy.

Smart was coming up close now, and Burnaby felt a quick stab of trepidation lest Smartarse got himself and the lads with him blown away. Odd how he could even think like that when all he was doing was rushing forward shooting, and flopping down to reload. Must be this damned command syndrome. Bullets spat and clacked about, and the smoke from the house started to swirl upwards in a thick black pall. Time to get up and run on again.

"Tom! They're chucking it in!"

Andy half-lifted, jerking his head savagely.

Burnaby looked.

Trampas stopped shooting.

A tiny space of silence opened out, with only the crackle of flames as a continuing background noise.

"Englishmen!"

The voice lifted from the knot of figures black against the snow outside the house. "Englishmen! Stop shooting!"

"Like hell!" said Spider.

"Hold it!" snapped Burnaby.

He yelled, hard and high: "Do you surrender?"

Almost no pause at all followed as the voice in good English yelled back. "Yes, yes. We surrender. Comrade."

"Kamerad," said Spider, and sniffed. "Bloody Argies wouldn't know a comrade if they hanged him."

"Which they do, from time to time," said Lawless. They were coming out of the manic possession of battle now, and feeling light-headed.

"We going to trust 'em?" demanded Andy. "You know what Smyjo said ... "

"We'll have to." Burnaby stood up. He felt exposed. "We've got to do this quick. Damned quick. Before they suss out how many of us there are – or aren't."

The other three of his patrol stood up alongside their leader. Burnaby took a breath and remained indifferent to the cutting clench of ice down his gullet.

"Throw down your weapons," he bellowed across. The white steam gouted out of his mouth. "Hands in the air. Do it *now*!"

Odd, damned eerie, how for a minute there he'd wanted to shout out: "*Schnell*!" That came from seeing too many war films.

He started to walk forward. He used his free hand to flip up the Scimitar.

"Q. Keep your heads down. Keep 'em covered. We're going in to take their surrender. But … "

All Q replied was: "Check."

Calling up Smart took a heart-stopping moment longer than he liked. Then:

"Yeah, Tom. They've had it. Caved in."

You couldn't say, though, Burnaby said to himself, you couldn't say without a fight. There were altogether far too many bodies lying about in the snow.

Smart went on: "Taff took a slug through his arm. In and out, lucky for him."

Instantly, Burnaby felt the ice-cold and the red-hot waves running through him. Suppose … ? He swallowed and snapped out: "Send Taff off to Sawbones, Smartie, right now."

"Check."

With that, Burnaby started to walk towards the blazing house. It seemed to him to take an interminable time to cross the snowy ground. For some idiotic reason he felt the cold striking up at him from his feet. Angrily, he kicked the notion away. Back in 1812 the Russians had put allspice in their boots to keep out the cold, and they'd knocked spots off old Boney. Allspice seemed to come only from Jamaica; well, maybe he'd have to try that one day. An unexpected burst of machine gun fire blasted from the front of the house.

Before he could speak the Scimitar said in Trampas's voice: "All cool. Some wallies thought they'd run off. They changed their mind."

My God! He'd been wandering along like a loon, dreaming random chaotic thoughts. "You didn't hit any?"

"No."

He was almost up to the corner and the group of

Argies. Most of them, but not all, had raised their hands. Burnaby let the rifle slide forward a little aggressively. Andy was breathing down his neck, and Spider and Lawless were up with them. The fire could be felt now – very cheering. Not quite what the owner would say. A damned expensive way of keeping warm he'd yell.

"Start shooing'em away from their weapons."

Smart's patrol joined in. The Argies were rounded up and the area cleared. As he looked at the dispirited men, Burnaby realized he had a task on his hands. He began to count them, unobtrusively, getting a quick approximation. Twenty – twenty-five, thirty, thirty-five.

Jeezus! What the hell did he do with them now?

First things first.

He yelled at the prisoners. "The man who shouted in English step forward. Is there a doctor here?"

Some of the wounded were screaming in a way that would bring Sawbones down like GFL – gee-eff-ell – greased lightning. A couple of men pushed their way out of the mass.

The doctor was instantly recognizable. He had a round well-fed face. He did not appear to be carrying any medical kit.

"Where's your first aid box?" demanded Burnaby.

The other fellow who wore captain's insignia replied. "The doctor does not speak English." This captain didn't look at all like a man who had just had his command shot from under him. He appeared perfectly at ease. He was alert, quick, and with a thick black moustache.

"Well, tell him to fetch it, quick. These poor devils must be attended to."

"Of course."

Then Sawbones was there, looking like murder.

"What about Taff?"

"Clean. Look at this bloody lot!"

Sawbones stared at the wounded men and then went

to work. In short order the Argentine doctor assisted. Using his head, Burnaby spoke to Andy and Smart. "Get the prisoners sorted out. Watch 'em all the time – you never do know."

Thwackers, in his mechanic's way, said: "Oh, these Latin types. They're all right when it comes to high-powered machinery. Look at their racing drivers. They're all flash. But when it comes to slogging – "

"They might," said Andy, "take it into their little pointy heads to duff us up when they see how many we are. So, watch it!"

Left Flank Wing remained out of sight, performing the task of providing defence to the force in case any benighted Argies turned up to find out what all the excitement was about.

Burnaby wirelessed to Spider to contact HQ and report what had gone on down here and to request assistance in handling the prisoners. He let the Argentine captain see him speaking into the handset, not what was said. Then, casually, he said to Andy, loud enough for the Argie to hear, "If anybody runs in or out they'll be blown apart by the rest of the company while we clear up here."

Andy played up. "The bloody lot of 'em don't know how lucky they are sitting up there while we do all the work." And, ferociously, to an Argentine trooper facing the wrong way: "Turn around, you monkey, feet apart, hands up in the air."

The searches were swift but thorough and an amazing assortment of lethal weaponry was produced. The age-old trick of carrying a few spare rounds in the hat lining was not overlooked. The Argies had revolvers, knives, grenades, all manner of offensive weapons stowed about their persons. All were removed and tossed on to a heap in the snow.

"Leave their personal kit. That's theirs."

"Check."

Looting was not a normal part of life in Strike Force.

The air of unreality persisted. Burnaby found the whole brief shooting match bizarre, even with his understanding of the nature of the combatants and of the apparently incredible events that could take place in the midst of battle.

He radioed up to Q. "Get on to Noggy and stir him up, will you, Q? We've got a real headache down here."

Q's reply astounded him.

"We've been on to Noggy. His answer is just coming in now... " A slight pause, and then Q said: "Spider says he heard it, and that Noggy said it. Apparently, Tom, they want you to march the prisoners in ... "

Burnaby did not say anything. Q's pause was quite deliberate, allowing Burnaby to come back with the burst of profanity or the appeals to a merciless God or whatever fashion his anger might take.

"Tom? You get that?"

"Yeah. I'm thinking."

If there was one particular item Burnaby did not want to get himself or the force into it was shepherding a bunch of Argie prisoners across this no man's land.

He wondered if he had an artful or an angry expression on his face as he spoke into the mike.

"We have a captain down here who was buddy-buddy with that guy Peter, who's going to do nasties back at GHQ. Tell 'em they'd better get him out of here quick. I can't take on these prisoners. If HQ don't make satisfactory arrangements I'll just have to turn 'em loose."

Q emitted a sound like a gas-geyser exploding.

"You would, too!"

"Too bloody right."

"I'll tell 'em. They might spare one Scout or Gazelle for this captain of yours."

"If they don't take 'em all off my hands, I'll just march off and leave 'em. We'll smash up all their weaponry first, of course."

"Oh – of course!"

CHAPTER FIFTEEN

In the event, HQ took the prisoners off Burnaby's hands. Even the brass hats weren't fool enough to keep tied up a group of personnel whom they no doubt thought of as a lethal bunch of maniacs. If Strike Force had been kept on the job of shepherding prisoners then the ancient Army practice of ramming square pegs into round holes, which in theory no longer existed, would be alive and rampant.

The house burned down, the farm buildings sloughing into shiny black chequers and drifts of grey ash. A few angles remained and the fireplace poked out ironically. When the snow eventually covered it all, it would look most romantic. Burnaby turned away in disgust.

This soldiering profession was a funny old business. You believed in certain values – and you put your fingers up at the modern cynics who thought values and virtues extinct – and yet you ended up with some poor sod's house burned down. Oh, well, Burnaby supposed vaguely that HMG would fork out for a new house.

They'd got on to the subject of soldiers when he and Anne had driven up to see Claire. He refused to let on that he was a Captain in R.Sigs, fully relishing the tartness of the reality that that was only a cover for his genuine work with Strike Force. As old Sergeant McArdle used to say in Catterick: "Irony is the educated man's boot in the crotch." He smiled, and Anne frowned.

"My grandfather was a padre on the Western Front.

He used to talk all round the subject."

"Nobody much talks about experiences like that."

The car ran well and all too soon they'd left the narrow leafy lane and were humming along the bypass. The road looked as though it had been dropped from on high and simply pushed everything out of the way to make room. Anne started in about soldiers and then stated a number of the more commonly held mistaken beliefs. In his guise as a dull businessman Burnaby forebore to correct her until she ranted on about the Americans. He knew she was far more of a fiery person than her drab exterior indicated, and he was dumbly expecting her to take the usual anti-American line on all manner of separate issues. She surprised him then.

"If it comes to a conventional Third World War I've no confidence in the Americans to hold off the Soviets."

"Oh?"

"Well, look! The Yanks can't fight for toffee. They shoot thousands of tons of shells to cripple one little Vietnamese and are too frightened to go out after him. Well, they ran away at Kasserine, didn't they? And look at the Battle of the Bulge! They're all mouth, the Yanks."

Burnaby controlled himself. So, okay, what Anne was saying was a lot of nonsense. The tragedy was that there were far too many people who believed it. Carefully, he tried to frame an answer. Before he could open his mouth she was rattling on. "And look at the Iranian hostage scene! Farcical – and look at our lads at the Iranian Embassy – "

"Look, Anne, you can't compare chalk and cheese. Anyway, if the Soviets should attack on the ground in Europe, which I hope to God never happens, the Americans have a slightly easier area to defend than we and the Jerries have."

"H'm. Fat lot of good – "

"No, wait. The Yanks had just got into the war, and

they were dropped on by veterans at Kasserine. Well, have you forgotten Dunkirk? And as for the Ardennes – good grief, girl, the Yanks did magnificently there!"

"Oh, yes, they trumpet that about Bastogne and the paratroopers holding out – "

"Surely, and rightly so. But after the initial flurry of panic, the Yanks got stuck in and did well. They are damned good fighting men. Anybody who forgets that is in for a shock."

She sat hunched away from him against the door. The light of evening faded in long lemon-coloured streamers. The lamps glowed spectral-like as they hit the first of the chain of high streets barring a quick run into London. Still, the traffic was not completely impossible and he wasn't into the business of pushing the car along as though there were no tomorrow.

He couldn't fathom Anne at all. She appeared dowdy; yet it was clear a spark smouldered there. He was beginning to think it was a spark of resentment. She liked to lash out. He defended the honour of various institutions when he considered that necessary. She was a mine of misinformation. Yet her adherence to the ideals of personal femininity gave an overall coherence to her beliefs so that she was not fooling herself, at least not consciously. On the subject of soldiering he told her a few hometruths about the gallantry of French and Italian soldiers, of their toughness and ability to fight. She did believe the Germans were the greatest soldiers, so he had no need to correct her there. Was all this her grandfather's doing?

When they talked about the video film Claire had taken part in, Burnaby felt again that amazement at her views. "It's only because Claire didn't want to make the film, Tom, that's all. There's nothing wrong with making love and if you want a record of that, why not?"

At this time he was navigating around the Elephant

and Castle and did not reply. He knew his way around here. "No, of course not. It's all a matter of free will. I agree it's up to Claire."

"Now," she said, and settled back with a tiny puff of air. "If I'd made the film – "

"You?"

"I'd show it to myself every day."

He shook his head. This was for real?

Just before they reached Claire's street Anne made some casual remark about Chelsea Barracks. Burnaby knew he had grown a trifle warm when they'd been talking about soldiers and he'd been correcting the common notion about the fighting abilities of the Yanks. When he'd spoken, an echo of his profession sounded in his own ears. Anne must have felt the same vibes, for as he turned into the street of three-storey tenement flats converted to swish apartments, she said: "The way you go on, Tom, anyone'd think you were a soldier. Look, there's Claire's place."

The street lamps existed in their individual haloes of golden-orange light. The plane trees still clothed themselves with leaves. There were few people about in this forlorn hour between day and night. Evening scents, powdery dust, engine oil, a whiff of smoke, the strange yet familiar scents of London town, all commingled on a summer day's dying. A white blot ran into the headlight's glare.

A figure, gesticulating, white and luminous from the car headlights, swelling and growing nearer with shocking speed. Burnaby hit the brakes and the car jumped and lurched forward before she stopped.

Anne said: "What – ? Oh, no … "

She had her door open and was out of the car before Burnaby slammed on the handbrake and jumped out.

In that harsh white pooling of light he saw the two girls as though entwined, entombed in marble, remote and monumental upon a pedestal. Anne cradled Claire. Her head bent down and the headlights caught at her hair and drowned her face in shadow.

The lights shone full upon Claire's face.

The bruises, blue and black and ochre yellow, like mustard smeared under blackberrry jam across her face, gave him a revulsion so fierce he gasped. He'd seen men with their guts hanging out, hadn't he? Well, why did this scene so shock and offend him?

"Claire ... " Anne was saying, hopelessly, over and over.

"The quickest thing now," Burnaby said as though drilling a squad in survival techniques, "is to take her to the hospital ourselves. Help me put her in the car."

Anne jerked upright at his tone.

He just didn't have time to do or think anything other than rush Claire to the place where trained people could help her. He was medically trained; he saw what was necessary. She had no broken bones, no internal injuries serious enough to cause her to bleed from the mouth or nose or ears. He picked her up, taking her out of Anne's arms, and carried her across to the car. Anne opened the rear passenger door and then got in beside her sister.

No one spoke. He drove to the hospital as though the car ran on tracks, barely conscious of turning the wheel or of changing gear. Claire was engulfed into the hospital casualty ward, and the liniment smell of the place wormed its way down Burnaby's gullet. He did not like hospitals, and yet thanked the Good Lord for them. They waited in silence, both, as Burnaby judged, wincing from the idea of what had happened.

When a man in a white coat whom Burnaby took to be a doctor appeared with news, everyone spoke at once.

Eventually they had it sorted out. There was extensive bruising and only a few cuts which would heal without scarring. Claire had not been marked. Burnaby followed

Anne and the doctor, feeling his way around his own emotions. No, of course not; no, they wouldn't mark her – not yet. She was too valuable – for now.

Swathed mummy-fashion, with holes for mouth, nostrils and eyes, Claire could be allowed to see them for five minutes. Anne was not crying; her face, when Burnaby noticed her as she bent over, looked fierce.

"Who did it, Claire? The police will want to know."

"No … police … "

Burnaby's guess was that the local factory would already have been informed and a young D.C. would be on his or her way around right now. If not sooner.

Claire's eyes moved in the white swathing. She tried to move her hand, her arm, and failed. Burnaby guessed she was attempting to grip his own arm to emphasize what she was trying to say. He bent closer.

"Yes, Claire?"

"Get – Tom – get the film … the vid – video – for me."

A pause accompanied by a sighing cough, a weak sound that even more upset Burnaby. The girl was badly injured and would have been in pain but for the drugs the doctor had used. She had been brutally punished. "Tom – get the film for me."

"Where is it?"

"Address in … handbag … "

The nurse bustled in and threw them out, but Burnaby had time to nod and attempt a smile and say: "I'll get the film, Claire."

Without speaking and in a subdued mood, Anne went with Burnaby to the car. As they entered, she looked across the steering wheel at him.

"Tom. So okay, you get the film. Then what?"

"Burn it."

"Then they'll do worse things to Claire."

"She paid them the money she owed. They did not return the film. They're in the wrong here."

"But they have – "

Thinking back to that moment, Burnaby found a weird and bizarre analogue of the Falklands mess. A group of people in the wrong had used force. If you used force to counter force, where did it all end? The King James Bible had mistranslated the first commandment. The Jewish version was: 'Thou shalt not murder', not: 'Thou shalt not kill'. But did killing ever end when you went on and on justifying it?

The problem presented to him over what he should do about Claire was weirdly relfected in what should be done about the Falklands. What seemed the perfectly obvious right course to pursue might easily turn out to be more disastrous than anyone could foresee. If you did nothing, then you had to live with the consequences of that. There was no doubt at all that the decision to send off brave young men to a mangey group of little islands down at the other end of the world had tapped an unexpected reservoir of enthusiasm in almost all the British people. It was, Burnaby supposed, like the one-time champeen of t' world trying to make a last come-back. Cruel analogy, maybe. But there was no mistaking the feeling that Britain had to knock in the Argies' back teeth before anything else. He remembered he'd thought he'd have to deal with the miserable bastards plaguing Claire ...

The coat-of-arms of the Falklands Islands, together with a sheep and the ship *Desire*, carried the motto: "Desire the Right". Yes, there were two ways of reading that. Thinking back as he crouched on tussocky grass watching a pack of enemy soldiers, Burnaby knew damn well which way the folk around here read it. Loud and clear.

The Argie soldiers below scurried about in their bulky padded anoraks as though they were Chinese re-fighting Korea. Sensible clothing when it got real cold, that, but when it got real cold what did the Argies do? Put on more vests and pants?

Strike Force had left the scene of their action, the burned-down farmhouse, the dead men to be buried, left all that to be cleaned up by the folk sent up from HQ. Their next task had been spelled out in the most simple terms.

After all – in one respect, weren't the men of Strike Force to be regarded as expendable?

Not, Tom Burnaby told himself with enormous vehemence, not with me, chum!

They caught up with the news.

Although odd rumours circulated around the reasons for the Welsh Guards having remained for a goodly length of time aboard *Sir Galahad*, the Guards had taken a nasty pasting and there were far too many fine young lads dead. Strike Force, although a hard and cynical outfit who killed and got killed in return, were perfectly capable of reacting with sorrow at this godawful news.

Still, this is what happens in war.

The Brits advanced to the east and a quantity of hard fighting from all the units immediately involved secured footholds on the surrounding hills on the avenue to Port Stanley. This was work that was fierce, hard, dangerous, work that demanded intelligence and skill as well as old-fashioned guts. To Burnaby's satisfaction, although not surprise, he realized the Brits were displaying all the necessary qualities.

The old champeen of t' world still had a lethal knock-out punch. The trouble there, of course, was that he did not have an unlimited supply.

Down below, the Argies were restless. They could hear the artillery pounding positions off to the flank and they could guess they'd come in for some stick before long. No soldiers like being bombarded by naval guns. The bluejackets shoot damn straight. And they have guns a damn sight bigger than the army's – even in today's popgun-armed ships compared with the battleships of a bygone era. Or so it always seems when the bricks start falling on your head.

Andy said: "Can you make out what they're up to, Tom?"

"Nope."

"Brown pants, I reckon," offered Spider evilly.

"You keep your eyeballs where they belong, Spider," reproved Andy in the mild tone that sent shivers up the back of hardened sergeants.

Spider switched around to check out the rear. No one wanted a case of British special forces shooting up British special forces, although it sometimes happened. There were now so many special forces operating on the shrinking area between the two opposing sides that some funny situations might arise. Like a fighting recce patrol of paras being told to clear off from here as the special forces had this patch.

Burnaby, right now, would have welcomed some para help. But the Maroon Machine was well committed now, storming hills, driving on, being heroes. Strike Force, Burnaby was seriously thinking, was on the thin edge of being burned out.

That little interchange just then wasn't like Spider ...

From their HQ Noggy kept on wirelessing fresh good news. Mount Harriet, Mount Longdon, Two Sisters, Goat Ridge, these were the stepping stones to Stanley being occupied – not without hard fighting – by the men who now just wanted to get to Stanley, get it over with, and go home.

Smyjo managed to contact Noggy and wirelessed a cautious statement that he was bored out of his skull, that the Vulcans had been raiding again, that everything was going well, and that Strike Force had not treated him at all well, not at all well, old son ...

Orders for the final series of assaults came through.

"Once we've cleared the final horseshoe of mountains," Burnaby told his men, feeling a trifle odd telling these veterans what to do, "we're home and dry."

"That's Tumbledown, Mount William and Wireless Ridge," said Q. "Right?"

"And Sapper Hill," Andy added.

Spider wanted to vent an evil spleen. "I'll tell you one thing. If Johnny Gurkha gets his kukri up 'em, they won't like it. They won't like it!"

"Right. Get your heads down." Burnaby did not even attempt a smile. He felt tired, dog-tired. "We're all ready for the off. I just hope it's our very last day of fighting in these islands."

CHAPTER SIXTEEN

The mortars went on firing just about all night. The weather was cold, but bearable. Snow clothed only the higher points; down in the valleys and along towards Stanley the going should not be too bad.

Spider's semi-humorous remark about the Gurkhas stayed with Burnaby as they waited for the off.

Yes, of course, Gurkhas were mercenaries; but they were not mercenaries in the more modern and unpleasant meaning of the word. They were, to all intents and purposes, a part of the British Army, as well as the Indian Army. Everybody liked Johnny Gurkha – unless you weren't on his side. To try to besmirch their upright character by calling them mercenaries and expecting people to fall about in horror was on a par with calling the Pope bad names for employing mercenaries.

Burnaby was not privy to the arrangements made by the general officer commanding for the morrow's attack; but it did not take a military genius to guess he'd put the Gurkhas along with the Scots Guards. The Gurkhas were reputed to work well with Scots, even unkilted ones.

So many times he'd lain half-awake and half-asleep, trying not to think about the dawn and what that would bring. How many of them would be killed? Perhaps Spider would fall, choking his guts out. Perhaps the Whizz Kid would be blown up by some infernal device not of his making. Perhaps ...

To hell with it!

He was a soldier and he had the finest bunch of tearaways there could be under his command. So sleep, get on with it tomorrow, and then sail home to sort things out with Claire and Anne ...

After the ups and downs of his relationship with the sisters Havisham, he wondered if he'd ever sort things out with them.

For a member of Strike Force breaking into the one-time shop premises had been a piece of cake. The burglar alarm was of the primitive kind, and a few careful snips with alligator clips removed its feeble menace.

The place had, until recently, been a delicatessen. Along with many of the older shops around Soho it had been abandoned and now served the newer industries of the area. The lingering odours of salami and garlic and würst seemed still to provide olfactory ghosts to haunt the place with memories of other days. Burnaby flashed his glim, found the right room, found the right cabinet after a search, drew forth the offending video cassette.

He held it in his hand, weighing it. Claire, when he'd visited her again, had been insistent that there was only the single copy in existence. It was here, in this video reproductive centre, to be copied. The long rows of video machines in the next room would each begin to receive images of Claire's naked body if the process was not squelched before it began.

As for her naked body, well, that had been on view for payment many times.

It was, decided Burnaby, what was done with and to that body that concerned Claire, and therefore him, at this moment. She had been violated, and, yes, it had been her own silly fault for gambling and piling up debts. Those debts had been paid, and the bastards still demanded her body.

Right.

At once Burnaby knew he was not going to enjoy this.

He plugged in the nearest video machine, watched the screen, slotted in the cassette.

He turned off the sound.

Mundane clothed actions between men and women started. Then some girls took off their clothes and frolicked on a lawn. Burnaby surmised this was the lawn and garden of the house where he had for a brief moment looked on as Claire was forced to take part. The action grew warm. He let the machine run. He took careful note of the timings.

When Claire walked on, did her stripping act, and then indulged in contortions with a variety of folk in a variety of positions, he checked the figures, rewound, and then set the machine to record, and wiped the lot.

He went through the whole tape like that, taking out every vestige of Claire's involvement, leaving everything else.

He didn't really see much of Claire, of her body, of what she was expressing. He saw a pinkly-white artefact, with crimson additions, moving about, and he wiped the slate clean.

Although the tape ran for only an hour and fifty-five minutes or so, the job took him longer than he'd anticipated. He was, of course, wearing skin-thin gloves. He slotted the cassette back in its cabinet, switched everything off, looked around, removed his alligator clips, and departed.

He had stolen nothing. He had done just the opposite; he had taken back stolen property.

Claire's body was her own. What she did with it was her decision. She had been forced into actions she did not wish to perform, force had been employed to make her do things repugnant to her. Now a modicum of force had been used to redress the balance. He went off back to

Claire's place where Anne was waiting up for him.

She was undecided, frightened, about what he had done.

"This doesn't solve anything, Tom! Now they'll tell Father – they threatened they would – "

"So they tell your father. He believes in his daughters, doesn't he? He'll ask Claire. If she loves the vicar then she'll lie. She'll deny it. The vicar will believe her. If that's the way of it – "

"But!"

"Or, she can tell the truth. Maybe your father will be able to handle it. Either way, whatever Claire decides, this will be finished."

"I'm not sure!"

"Nor am I. All I know is Claire had something stolen from her against her will. Now we've taken that back. If those bastards want to make something more of it, then – "

"They will!"

"Then we'll deal with that when and if it happens."

He went around to the little hotel at which he was putting up for this visit, a clean and relatively comfortable if unambitious establishment, and caught up with his sleep.

As promised, mid-morning next day he returned to the flat where Anne was expecting him.

The front door was ajar.

Frowning, he went in quietly, padding along the carpeted hallway.

The low rumble of voices grew louder as he approached the lounge. Quietly, he peeked through the crack of the half-open door.

He could see two men, parts of them, standing in sharp suits and polished shoes. He waited, listening.

"So we wait for this character to come back."

"I'll nail his ears to the floor!"

"Now, now, Tony. Is that nice? Let's hear what he has to say first."

Burnaby started to sweat. If they knew about him, what had they done to Anne to make her tell? He couldn't see her; but he could hear a distressing sobbing.

"Go and take a look, Bugs – "

The voice, metallic, accented, did not finish the sentence. The door jerked fully open. A man stood there, a large hairy man wearing a fur-trimmed leather jacket, with a quantity of gold chains and rings. In his fist he held a pistol.

With the sudden opening of the door, that pistol pointed directly at Burnaby's midriff.

The man with the pistol, who had to be called Bugs, yelped.

"Hey, boss – !"

"I see him." The metallic voice sounded genuinely pleased. "Come in, punk, and don't do anything foolish. Bugs would love to fill you full – "

Burnaby guessed the man was acting. He had a thin and sallow face decorated by a narrow black moustache, and his every mannerism bespoke a man fixated on gangster movies. Black and white gangster movies.

There was a fourth man in the room, clad in jeans and T shirt under a windproof. This man now took out a flick knife. If the man with the pistol and the man with the knife were the hired help, then the other one in the suit could be the accountant, and the sallow-faced speaker the boss. Maybe he was the brains. At any event, they had Burnaby nicely caught.

He looked across the lounge towards the settee. Anne sat hunched up in her dowdy flowery dress, sobbing. He could not see any marks on her face.

She stared up at him. Her eyes looked brilliant and enormous.

"Tom! They made me – "

"That's all right – "

Bugs, the fellow with the Beretta 9mm fitted with a silencer, jerked the pistol and, obligingly, Burnaby moved further into the room. Tony, the other fellow in the sharp suit, said: "You may have ruined that film, smart guy. We'll take it out of your hide – "

"Now, now, Tony." The boss, in his role as a black and white movie ganster, was clearly enjoying this. That got up Burnaby's nose. "Don't frighten him. Oh, sure, we'll take it out of him. And we'll make another film, better this time than the last."

Anne jerked to her feet. She looked a mess.

"I've told you! I'll act in the film! I want to!"

The men laughed at her.

"You old bag? Look at you!"

"I don't mind! It's not only Claire – "

Although these unpleasant men couldn't see it, Burnaby could. He recalled what Anne had said before. She believed in what she was saying, and she hungered for the chance to parade as her sister did, to perform in a film, to be watched and lusted after.

"Shut your face, you stupid bitch." The boss waved her away.

Anne drew a breath. Her hair, fallen away from that severe bun, swirled about her head. She reached up a hand to the neck of the dress.

"I can do it! I can! Look!"

Her hand ripped down. Buttons sprayed. In a swift and fluid motion she ripped the dowdy old dress down and stepped out of it. Burnaby blinked.

Well, now ...

Anne Havisham, drab little sister of the gorgeous Claire, wore startling underclothes. Amazing. A vivid scarlet, edged in black lace. The bra uplifted her breasts, leaving the nipples exposed. She had large and well-formed breasts. A frilled suspender belt and narrow black suspenders upheld sheer nylon stockings. But the panties! They were open, scarlet, daring, flaunting, completely unexpected. She lifted herself and posed, and, indeed, she had a figure that was most appealing, narrow waisted and flared of hip.

Bugs with the gun turned his head and gawped.

In that instant Burnaby was on him.

He just missed the grab at the pistol which sailed up in an arc and descended to skid and vanish under the sideboard.

The knife merchant yelped and jumped in. Burnaby hit Bugs behind the ear; but, again, because of the knife attack, missed a clean blow. Bugs stumbled forward. The knife man held the knife low, the right way around, and Burnaby had to forearm that way, sidestep and put two fingers up the fellow's nostrils. Maybe that wasn't the best use of his comprehensive knowledge of keninja, the system of unarmed combat and a distillation of the best of the martial arts taught within Strike Force. But it served for now.

The fellow dropped the knife, screaming, reeling away with with dark ruby-red blood beginning to drop from his ripped nostrils.

Tony, anxious to pin Burnaby's ears to the floor, rushed in and Burnaby swivelled, kicked him in the groin, and then started in on Bugs. Bugs was big and tough and fancied himself. His blows went everywhere except to land on the target. When Burnaby had hit him enough he gave him a final chop and Bugs went down to slumber on the carpet.

Anne called: "Tom! He's going for the gun!"

The boss was on his hands and knees scrabbling under the sideboard. He swivelled a face now haggard with fear.

Burnaby walked over and kicked him in the ear.

He took a breath and looked around.

"We'd better call the police – "

"Oh, Tom!"

She was on him, raging. Her moist lips slobbered all over his face, she was clawing and clutching at him.

"Love me, Tom! Make love to me! Please! Now!"

Inflamed by the passions aroused in her she began to rip off those gaudy undergarments, although in all truth they revealed little more when they were off than they had done when on. He held her off.

"Stop it! Anne!"

Her hair swirled over her face. Her eyes were wide and staring. Her lips, red and moist, opened convulsively. Her tongue darted over them like the tongue of a snake.

"Tom! Quick! Quick!"

Naked, she flung herself forward, clawing for him. So he had to slap her around the face. He did not like doing that. But it was a cure.

She sagged back, crying. She folded her arms across her chest, and crumpled up on the settee. Burnaby picked up the discarded dress and threw it at her.

"Not now, Anne, and not like this. Now, let's get the police."

Her gaze followed him across to the phone.

"What kind of businessman are you?" She began to make a gesture at the four recumbent men, and then drew her arm back across to cover herself. "What are you, a merchant of death?"

"No," said Burnaby, sharply. "Quite the reverse."

Now, looking at the Argie positions they had to neutralize, he knew that to be absolutely true. He had no wish to kill anyone. That he had to from time to time was a part of a greater whole. He just wanted these Argie idiots rounded up and shooed off the Falklands. Then they could all go home.

West of Stanley Four Five Commando had taken Two Sisters and southwards Four Two Commando took

Mount Harriet. The Scots Guards went forward to slog a very tough battle for Tumbledown. The Argies, sensible for once, did not hang around when the Gurkhas appeared but legged it immediately. This annoyed the Gurkhas. To the north and west, Three Para was moving forward after Mount Longdon. To the north Two Para put in a noisy and brilliantly lit action to swarm across Wireless Ridge. The ring closed in on Stanley.

Strike Force hacked along a narrow track around a hillside ready to continue the advance. For Burnaby, the fighting came in spurts, as though a part of a bad dream. Some of the Argies ran off immediately the Brits appeared. But a large number stayed, holed-up in sangars and bunkers, and resisted with courage and tenacity.

"Winkle the buggers out," said Burnaby. "We're not here to indulge in grand fire fights."

So far no one had been hurt. This was a miracle, for there were altogether too many snipers with expensive American sighting equipment picking off anyone foolish enough to expose himself. Andy got himself into a little sniper-hunting operation, and bagged one, and no one had time to stop and congratulate him. It was on and on, push forward, get the buggers on the go.

As they moved forward they found some areas where the ground was its usual soft peaty self, and others where it was damned hard. Watching every step of the way, Burnaby was well aware that Strike Force was playing a tiny, almost insignificant part in these greater events. Now it was time for the Paras, the Commandos, the Guards and the Gurkhas. They were an elite force, if ever there was one.

Then a rotten infuriating bloody sniper shot him.

Burnaby felt a bang on the inside of his left forearm. Instantly, he dropped. His left arm refused to support him and he rolled awkwardly sideways to the right. He felt no pain yet, and was aware of Spider shrugging off the big radio cursing away to himself in a vicious monotone, and of him and Lawless vanishing off to the right. Andy went to the left.

Shortly thereafter a series of bangs and sundry crashes lit the sky.

Spider came back, with Lawless, and Andy rejoined.

By that time Sawbones was there.

"Nothing, Tom. Straight through the fleshy part. You'll live. Have to strap you up, though – "

His arm felt numbed, yet it ached damnably.

"If you must, Sawbones, do it so I can rest my rifle – "

Sawbones sniffed. But he strapped Burnaby's arm so that the Personal Weapon could still be fired.

When the news came over the wireless that white flags had been seen, that reports spoke of Stanley flying hordes of white flags everywhere, Burnaby felt a weird drifting of his spirits. This was what he had longed for. So it was here. Why wasn't he leaping up and down and cheering like everyone else?

Maybe a recollection that the Havisham sisters' ordeal hadn't really finished with the arrival of the police had a great deal to do with it.

Two Para was tabbing into Stanley, and the Commandos were yomping in, so Burnaby decided that it would be a good idea to go along and see what was what.

Sawbones wanted to be tiresome about Burnaby's wound.

"Okay, Tom, so it's a clean shot through. But wounds can do funny things if you don't take care. You don't want to lose the use of that arm, do you?"

"You've done your tricks on me, Sawbones. It don't feel as though I've an arm here – "

"Precisely, you benighted idiot!"

"Well, there's not much more we can do, is there, right

now? The quicker we get into Stanley the quicker we can get me to the hospital. But, Sawbones, you may not believe this; but I have great trust in you."

"Ha!"

The last hike into town did not seem real.

This was the objective for which vast sums of money had been spent, for which men and woman had slaved around the clock, and for which men had died.

Burnaby refused to be rushed. He was cheered by the sight of red berets going in. Trust the paras to get their helmets off and the red berets on sharpish!

The roads were wet. The place held a cheerless air. Strike Force would find themselves a nice cosy billet for the night. A fierce snowstorm blew up and dissipated. News trickled out. Menendez had made a formal surrender, the GOC had had a traumatic flight in by chopper through the snowstorm, it was all over, the paper was signed, they could go home.

There were Argies all over town, roaming among the little wooden and corrugated-iron-roofed houses. Most of them still lugged their weapons along, not knowing what to do. Paras and Marines were out rounding them up and piling up rifles and machine guns in enormous heaps here and there, filling trucks with them. No one seemed quite to grasp what was exactly happening, although this was clearly a mistaken impression. After a surrender of this magnitude, when more men surrender to less, it inevitably took time to sort out the mess.

Burnaby refused to go along to one of the hotels and join the roisterers. He had Strike Force to see to. They wanted to keep him in the hospital, along the coast road by the Secretariat. He had Sawbones with him, and a frown and a curt refusal, although perhaps wounding to the nurses who were ecstatic at the arrival of the British, got him off the hook and out of it. His place was with Strike Force. This, at least, he owed to the Major.

Q had taken the men off to a comfortable billet he had commandeered in one of the abandoned houses. Sawbones walked out of the hospital, shivered, said: "You'd best get some shut-eye, Tom. Let's go along to – "

"All right. It's not far."

They turned right by the Secretariat towards Ross Road. Government House lay behind them to the west. At that, Burnaby would welcome the chance to put his head down and sleep and forget all the horror and the cold and the pain.

People were moving about. Some civilians were out looking on, and no doubt the kelpers would stream in from the camp now. There did not seem to be any Argies about, but British soldiers showed going about their lawful duties. A knot of figures moved along towards the road leading off to the government jetty where a few ships lay tied up.

Sawbones said: "Hullo! There's Smyjo!"

Burnaby stared where the doctor pointed.

Sure enough, there was Smyjo, advancing towards them, beaming all over his face. He raised a hand in greeting.

"What the hell are you doing here, Smyjo?"

"Trying to find you, old boy. It's all over now – "

"And the general?"

"Oh, he's frightfully busy. A kind of triumphal procession. He told me to clear out and rejoin my unit. So here I am."

"Did – ?"

Smyjo brushed that erect and military forefinger over his upper lip.

"Not a sign, old son. Nary hair or hide of him. If you ask me, that Peter who wanted to be an assassin is safely in the bag."

"Well, we're off to our billet. We're knackered."

"I'm with you. Plenty of time for celebration."

Farther along the knot of men appeared a dark mass. A few paras, going the other way, saluted. From the side of the road a captain in R.Sigs appeared. Looking at him, Burnaby felt a sudden flash of irritation. These signals wallahs who clamped around their wireless sets at HQ keeping in touch with the world were no doubt highly important and valuable. Yet, as in this case, here they were out sorting over what there was of loot. This specimen toted a jimpy. The General Purpose Machine Gun was slung over his shoulder, angled slightly, and the belt of ammo draped over his arm and up over his shoulder.

Also, so Burnaby saw, he had a couple of grenades fastened American fashion to his pockets. How these behind-the-lines boys fancied themselves!

"Well, old boy," Smyjo was saying, "our job's done. The general's safe. They're taking poor old Menendez out to *Fearless*. Got to handle him right – "

Burnaby saw the Royal Signals captain raise the machine gun, half-turning. He saw his face. It was Peter, the Anglo-Argentinian with a murder mission.

Instantly, what Smyjo had said as they eavesdropped on that secret conversation made sense. The covert understanding of orders that would be obeyed only if the worst came to the worst. For the Argies, things had come to the worst.

Failing to do the job he had started to do, Peter was now obeying those secret and covert orders. If he was successful ... Burnaby wasn't worried a single bit about imbecilic notions of South American honour and *machismo*. He saw what the world would say, how world opinion would blame and condemn the British.

Britain would stand before the bar of world opinion as the callous murderer of a beaten general.

"Peter!"

He called it out, loud and clear. As the man, shocked, swung about, Burnaby somehow balanced his rifle across his wounded arm. The muzzle did not hold steady.

"Peter! It's no good. It's too late."

"What the hell!" Smyjo raked around for his SMG.

The Anglo-Argentine's maching gun was not yet up; it still snouted at an angle to the ground.

Burnaby shouted again.

"If you lift that jimpy I'll kill you."

Then, just to make sure, he yelled: "Put the machine gun down, Peter."

"Kill the bastard and have done," roared Smyjo. The noise of the bolt going back as he cocked the SMG sounded like a railway train colliding with a steel wall.

"Hold it, Smyjo! There's been enough killing."

"But – "

"Stand fast!"

Then, again, trying to speak reasonably, Burnaby called across: "Peter. We know about you. We know what you have been ordered to do. But it's not worth it. Not now. You'll come out of this with honour. Don't foul it all up now."

The man's machine gun trembled as he swung fully about. Burnaby wasn't at all sure he could hit the blighter with a wounded arm interfering with his aim. The thick moustache had been neatly trimmed and looked most English. Again Burnaby was struck by the force of personality in the man's face, its handsomeness, the determination and resolution.

"How do you know? You *cannot*!"

"But I do, Peter. If you murder your own general, be very sure you will not blame us. I can't guarantee to shoot straight. I can't guarantee to wing you. If I shoot – and I'll shoot long before you get that jimpy into action – you're likely to be very badly wounded, gutshot, or malletted."

The vicious power in Burnaby's own words shook him. He could feel this situation, could feel the ramifications. They all stood there, held by hatred and determination to conquer, to redeem honour, to do the right thing. Burnaby poised to shoot.

The clump of figures up ahead moved on unaware of the deathly struggle of will. Now they were out of grenade range. That, at least, was a beginning.

"You cannot win," Burnaby said. "Is your life worth it? Put the machine gun down and put your hands up and if you make a wrong move I'll shoot you down. I don't believe you're a mad dog; but if you persist in acting like one then you'll leave me no alternative."

A shudder in that powerful figure, a trembling of the machine gun – and then Peter bent and slipped the sling from his shoulder, and stood back with the jimpy at his feet. He put his hands in the air.

Smyjo breathed out. Then he said: "Watch the bugger's grenades, Tom. You know what Andy says ... "

"Oh, you can deal with him now, Smyjo. Clap him in some lock-up and tell the security lads. He can go with the other prisoners, I think."

Smyjo looked at Burnaby. "You all right, Tom? Your wound?"

"Perfectly, thank you, Smyjo."

Smyjo, SMG held aggressively, nodded and marched over to the Anglo-Argentinian. Just before they moved off Burnaby shouted: "Peter. You were very lucky I did not shoot you. I did not want to kill you, even though you deserved it, I think. You behaved yourself in the end. If you try anything like that in the future, play silly buggers again, then, believe me, you will be shot."

When Smyjo had marched the prisoner off, Sawbones said: "It's all over, Tom. We've liberated the Falklands, even though ... "

"I know. Even though the future doesn't look promising. But, right now, we've done it. And I'm going to put my head down and sleep for a week."

Then he'd go home and see what was going to happen with Claire and Anne Havisham. That could wait.

He could not see the flag the liberating forces had raised again. The Falklands Islands flag, the Union Jack with the badge in the centre. But he knew what the badge said, and that about summed it all up.

"Desire the Right."

Also available in this series:

SS PANZER BATTALION
DEATH'S HEAD
CLAWS OF STEEL
GUNS AT CASSINO
THE DEVIL'S SHIELD
HAMMER OF THE GODS
FORCED MARCH
BLOOD AND ICE
THE SAND PANTHERS
COUNTER-ATTACK
SLAUGHTER GROUND
HELLFIRE
FLASHPOINT

HIMMLER'S GOLD
Stormtroop 5

Leo Kessler

BLOOD MONEY . . .

1944. The Allied stranglehold on Hitler's Germany tightens amid the flames. But in Himmler's mind, the dream of a thousand-year Reich lives on . . .

Dedicated to continuing the Führer's battle, he needs to transport a fortune in diamonds to South America. He needs an elite team, hardened in the most merciless arenas of conflict, to carry them across a Europe rent by war. He needs Stormtroop Edelweiss.

Until Stuermer's men, the dirtiest dozen of them all, begin to make a few plans of their own . . .

Futura Publications
Fiction/War
0 7088 1843 9

FIRE OVER KABUL
Stormtroop 6

Leo Kessler

1942: 'GENTLEMEN, I WILL NOW TELL YOU HOW WE WILL CRUSH THE ENGLISH!'

And so, Colonel Stuermer, C.O. of Germany's elite reconnaissance and assault company, Edelweiss, learns of their next mission. At *Reichsführer* Himmler's command, Stormtroop Edelweiss are to travel over treacherous terrain in hostile lands to make the inaccessible, accessible. Pioneering a route from Kabul in neutral Afghanistan, through impenetrable mountains in Nepal, dank rain forests in Assam, Stuermer and his men will herald the liberation of India. For the Germans – using Edelweiss's matchless skills – and their Jap allies have promised the Indian people their freedom . . .

Futura Publications
Fiction/War
0 7088 2223 1